D1084824

the struggle for happiness

ALSO BY RUTHANN ROBSON

FICTION:
Eye of a Hurricane
Cecile
Another Mother
a/k/a

NONFICTION:
Legal Issues for Lesbians and Gay Men
Lesbian (Out)Law: Survival Under the Rule of Law
Sappho Goes to Law School: Fragments in Lesbian Legal Theory

POETRY:
Masks

the STRUGGLE *for* HAPPINESS

RUTHANN ROBSON

ST. MARTIN'S PRESS ☰ NEW YORK

This is a work of fiction. Names, characters, places, and incidents either are a product of the author's imagination or are used fictitiously, and any resemblance to actual persons, living or dead, events, or locales is entirely coincidental.

Design by Mspace / Maura Fadden Rosenthal

ISBN 0-312-25219-6

First Edition: April 2000

10 9 8 7 6 5 4 3 2 1

contents

the struggle for happiness

black squirrels

*T*he beautiful days are the worst.

The bitter blue of the sky. The sun glaring like an interrogation spotlight: Confess every crime; betray every accomplice. The innocent green of the trees hiding the terrible spores and pollens and industrial chemicals that make me sneeze and ache and cry.

Although for a moment, sometimes, when the temperate breezes have massaged me into a state of relaxation, the sky and the sun and the trees all possess a majestic clarity. But resplendence is always sharpened by impending loss. Witness Alexis. She had never looked more desirable than the last time I saw her, our belongings segregated into hers and not-hers in our on-the-market apartment. The apartment had also never looked more inviting, its countertops gleaming from Windex and the lack of clutter of daily living.

But this is more serious.

This is the planet.

Though most people don't see it; don't perceive that the earth is dying, gasping and thrashing.

Maybe it's the pleasantness that prevents people from comprehending. Days like these, perfect as five-for-a-dollar postcards, lull people into thinking that everything is fine. The sky is nothing other than wallpaper: embossed with clouds and uniformly blue. The sun a gently swaying chandelier; the trees coat racks of green jogging suits. Instead of sharpening perceptions, people get dull. Insensate. That's what beauty does. I should know. I wrote a book on it: *Aesthetics and Argument in Women's Literature.*

I also used to teach a course by the same title. And one called "Identity in Twentieth Century Manuscripts." And one named "The Sex of Text." And every fifth semester, in the democratic departmental rotation, I would be assigned "Survey" or even "Composition." Although it didn't really matter what the course was titled. I always taught the same thing, only the context varied. Literary criticism according to Derrida. Take a text and twist it inside out. I guess I was effective, or at least entertaining. I was a popular professor. My enrollments and student evaluations told me so.

Despite all the pronouncements about the death of deconstructionism, it was thriving at what we called Cool U.

And I was thriving.

Although, of course, I didn't think so.

I thought I was riddled with neuroses. In another era, I would have used words such as *angst* and *existential*. In this era, no labels were necessary. In fact, no labels were permitted. To describe was to court imperialism, annulling all the referents that went unexpressed by one's statement. I achieved an enviable level of vagueness, but I used very important and precise words in discussing this vagueness.

But my main weapon in my struggle to be happy was my secret box.

Handmade paper, ten by twelve, and a cover with flaps lovingly diapered over the exposed slits. Baby blue, like worn and well-loved jeans the moment before the knee is about to rip. And as soft. Even the nubs are soft. Inviting as any fantasy: A lover (in her torn-at-the-knee jeans) sits on a couch; my face is on her thigh, my cheek rubs against the pulls in the warp of the thin denim.

It was expensive, purchased at one of those trendy papier

shops, and it wore a deep blue velvet necklace to conceal its cleavage. It was difficult to violate its virginity with the first piece of paper, but eventually I stuffed it with a motley assortment of mementoes that might convince me I was valuable, appreciated, and loved. There were thank-you notes from students, expressing their feelings that I had made a difference in their educations, if not their lives. There were a few photographs of me in the company of people who were prominent and smart and voguishly controversial. An acceptance letter from a semiprestigious journal and my first and second book contracts. An anniversary card from Alexis.

When I was feeling what I called underappreciated, I could lift the lid of my baby-blue box and have a tangible argument that my feelings were a brand of self-pity rather than a glimpse of truth. It had not been enough when I was denied tenure. Or not denied, according to the chair of the committee, but advised to withdraw my application. I don't think I consoled myself with the contents of my box even once during those dreadful two years when I felt that everyone at my second-rate university thought I was third rate. But after another—more traditional—book and another application, my baby-blue box could boast the formal university letter awarding me tenure.

Tenure: success.

It felt like failure, of course, but it was success.

It all changed with the accident.

Not that it was an accident. To call it an accident negates the intentionality involved. The gross negligence, as my attorney would say. The sheer cruelty of it.

To call it an accident makes it seem sudden. Like a lightning bolt on a crystal-clear day. Or like an automobile driving through the plate-glass front of my favorite bookstore, where I had been standing on line, waiting to purchase the newest translation of something or other. Like a rat bite.

Instead of a seeping reality.

I had expected Alexis to come up here once in a while. To

bring me some lasagna and gossip from the city. It isn't a far drive, not really, or that's what she used to say when she wanted to escape the cement summer of the city. That's what she had argued when she had wanted to buy this cottage as our vacation home. I had wanted to be on the beach, preferably in a gay resort: to be surrounded by surf and sand and women holding hands. She had snorted, as if I was being impractical. She said something about tax rates and disaster insurance costs. The numbers were on her side; they always were. I didn't even argue. I let her win.

"Isn't it lucky we got the cottage in the country?" she said after the accident. After we were splitting up and splitting everything. After the doctors said I needed to live in a more pristine climate, away from the city if possible.

"The beach would have been better," I said. I no longer wanted to let her win.

Still, I suppose I thought it would not be a far drive now; I suppose I thought she would want to check up on me. But she hasn't been here even once. She did help me move out of the apartment and arranged for some of her students to help me move in here. Move my clothes and my books and my desk and my computer. Which was nice of her. Very nice. It was amicable, really. She got the proceeds from the apartment and I got the country cottage. She got an offer from the mathematics department at a more prestigious university and I got disability payments. It all seemed so sensible, so fair, so fucking rational.

I'm sure I depress her. Hell, I depress myself. It's better not to think about her. Forget any speculations: Forget *shoe;* forget *other foot;* forget *if.*

It isn't as if the accident were her fault. It was just synchronicity.

I didn't used to believe in such things as the possibilities of patterns in nature. Not patterns. Not nature. I was poststructuralist, postromantic. But sitting on my deck all day watching the squirrels weave through the woods has changed my perspective about a lot of things. Including Alexis.

I'm glad she left me.

She is a selfish, shallow twit. Smart, certainly, but without depth. When I tried to talk to her about environmental degradation, she exhaled that superior-sounding sigh she had perfected in our years together. I think that was the last time she telephoned me. The irises had just been starting to unfold their brief but purple existence. I was talking to her on the portable phone, sitting on the deck, enjoying the sun.

She laughed, a sour little laugh, and told me I should think about other things.

Like what? Like the day I won't be able to slide the sliding-glass doors open and get out on the deck at all? Like this morning, leaning on the bathroom wall so I wouldn't fall and trying to pull my pants down fast enough so I didn't piss all over myself? Like trying to open the refrigerator?

I didn't say any of these things, of course.

Not because I wasn't thinking them or feeling hateful enough to say them, but because I didn't want her pity.

Didn't want to imagine her getting off the phone and turning to her new girlfriend, the artiste, with a significant tear gleaming in her left eye (her left eye always teared first) and getting comforted. Like she was the one who was sick.

It was probably that day or the next that I finally called Helping Hands, as suggested by my new physician and my social worker. I didn't want strangers in my little house, but I realized that Alexis wasn't going to be here to help. And even if she were, she had become a stranger, so what was the difference?

Linda was a student, she explained. Mountain Community and Technical College. Doing an internship at a home-service organization, Helping Hands. Working nights as a security guard, Protection Unlimited.

And sometimes she was pretty tired. Once she fell asleep on my couch, still wearing her green uniform. And I let her sleep there. While I maneuvered myself through the sliding-glass doors onto the deck and sat in the sun, looking at the weeds grow around the tomato plants. On a good morning, I could get myself into the garden. It was hell bending over without fainting, so I would lie down on one of the boards between the rows of plants and pull up those dreadful things Linda told me were called purslane, dropping them into a bucket. Then I'd slide forward and weed some more. It wasn't relaxing, but it kept me from thinking about next summer's garden and how I would ever manage to plant anything.

An hour of weeding usually sent me to bed for the rest of the day. Once, I fell into bed before I could manage to take a shower. I woke up smelling like tomato plants, the summer sun slanting deep in the hollows of the mountains.

On a really good morning, I can drive. I get myself over to the Nissan pickup, then scramble in the door. I catch my breath and always count to ten before I turn the key. Backing up is a real drain on my energy, but once I'm on the road, usually everything is fine. It's the destination that is the biggest problem. How to slide out of the truck in the grocery store parking lot while looking natural? I'm terrified that someone is going to come over and ask me if I need help, but no one ever does. I always try to park close to a grocery cart, so I can use that for support. And I always bring my three-pronged cane, hooked on the metal cart like an explanation to all those unasked questions.

And yes, it usually sends me to bed for the rest of the day. I am careful never to buy anything that needs to be cooked that night. I plan ahead and buy something from the take-out deli in the back of the store.

And yes, I always wonder whether I will be back as I look at the produce section for what might be the final time. The apples gleam green and red and yellow, absolutely resplendent.

I have taken to lying to Linda. About going to the grocery store, because she will yell at me if she figures out I've made the ten-minute drive to the Grand Union. But about other things too. Things that don't matter. Not to her. Not to me. Telling her that Alexis just telephoned, for example. Or that my parents are dead. Or that a black squirrel ate a nut right from my hand.

It helps me pass the time.

It helps me convince myself that I am still interesting, still fascinating. That I still have a life worth living.

It helps me to ignore the carcasses of my frost-crucified tomato plants, their withered limbs hanging on the galvanized steel of their cages, begging me for a decent burial in the compost pile.

It helps me to ignore the songs of the birds, entreating me to fill the squirrelproof feeder with sunflower seeds, now on sale in those inconsiderate five-pound bags at the Grand Union.

The cold weather is descending rapidly. It seems unnatural. I guess because I had never stayed here except in June or July; for me it was a place of only summer. Yes, there had been that one Thanksgiving—the year I was waiting for the decision in my first tenure application—Alexis and I had driven up here. Snubbing the Grand Union, we had brought all of our groceries from the city: a kosher roasting chicken, rosemary and lemons, oysters and bread for stuffing, and some exotic gravies. We had made a delicious dinner, pretending in some subtle way, I suppose, that we were in the French countryside. Provence, perhaps. Though without the sun. It was so gray that the security lights stayed on all day, their motion detectors activated by the leaves whirling in the wind.

We drank a woody red wine and read our books. I recall I was reading the newest translation of Helene Cixous. I don't remember what Alexis was reading, though it was probably some book of equations. I do remember that I looked up from my pages and right there at the sliding-glass door had been a pair of eyes looking back at me.

"A mink!" I stage-whispered to Alexis.

She put down her book. "I don't think so," she said. "It might be a rat. But I think it's just a squirrel."

It didn't look like the squirrels in the city, I thought, at least the ones I saw in the little triangle of dirt called a park that huddled near our apartment building. Those animals were smaller and had vague tails. They also ran around in circles, which Alexis said reminded her of me. I thought she was teasing, but she began to say it every time we passed them. She said it so much I started to hate those damn squirrels.

"Squirrels are gray," I reminded Alexis, not wanting this

beautiful, sleek creature to be the same as those city animals she used as an excuse to mock me.

"Maybe it's a mutant," she answered. By now the animal had scampered off the deck, past the garden, and back into the woods.

"Or a different brand?"

"Brand?" she laughed. "You mean breed, don't you, baby?"

"It's the wine." I giggled.

"Have some more." She rose to fill my glass.

"It could be a mink," I said.

"It wasn't." She shook her head. "Though I'm sure you want to think it was." She kissed me as she handed the wineglass back to me.

I vowed to do some research when we got back to the university.

"I didn't know you liked little soft and furry animals," she teased, but her voice was gentle. She reached for the bottoms of the aubergine silk pajamas I was wearing—an anniversary present from her—and untied the belt. My pajama bottoms threatened to puddle at my ankles.

She did that for the rest of the weekend. She would laugh and I would laugh and I thought that laughter would echo through the cottage and through our lives forever.

Or at least I didn't think it would stop so soon.

After I was advised to withdraw my tenure application, things got a little difficult.

But it was worse after I was granted tenure.

Throughout everything, I was popular as a professor; I still had a few students who wrote me thank-you notes; still had overenrolled classes and overflowing office hours. Though once I was tenured my students had to come to see me in another building. In the basement of another building. Nothing personal. A row of faculty offices was being made into an administrative suite. My office, of course, was in that row.

"Re: Restructuring," the memo from the chair of the department read.

I tried not to believe I was being punished for getting tenure.

My new office, windowless and small, was in the Sciences building, cuddled between the Zoology Lab and the Small Mammal Research Development Office. It was always empty in the corridor, in the early morning when I came to work, and even in the middle of the afternoon. In the evenings and on weekends, it was positively ghostly. It was almost as if I had the whole floor to myself.

I took me a while to arrange my books on the shelves. I put my blue box in a place I thought it would be safe and bought a fluorescently purple Indian bedspread to cover the metallic desk. I started toying with doing something creative, now that I finally had tenure. I was thinking of inverting narrative by rewriting that classic narrative of inversion, *The Well of Loneliness*. But I couldn't get past rereading the first three pages about the birth of the character I would call Stevie without succumbing to a desperate headache.

I thought it was *The Well*. Such an intimidating choice. Who the hell was I to try to render it as a poststructuralist text? But I had dissected my plan into pieces: I would set it in the United States, make its discourse of identity much more contemporary, give the beloved Mary a voice, and have it have a happy (if indeterminate) ending. My ideas sounded plausible inside my own head, but I could not get them to float on the computer screen no matter how long I tried to focus on the letters that stayed still only if I squinted.

I started getting stomach aches. I blamed caffeine. Now that I did not have access to the coffeepot in the English department mail room, I was drinking more coffee, not less. I had bought a small coffee maker for my office and made myself a cup as a substitute for the conversation I could have gotten in the mail room. And then another cup.

If I was the kind of person given to self-pity, I would have complained of being lonely.

One night I fainted. Although for a while I convinced myself I had fallen asleep. Wiped the vomit from between the plastic squares of my keyboard with tissues folded strategically. Told Alexis I had been working hard. Making progress on my new book. I can't recall whether she seemed to believe me or not to care.

It was just malaise, I told myself.

I was overworked and underappreciated and stressed out.

Friends prescribed a sabbatical. But the university had suspended them because of the budget situation. I tried not to dwell on the fact that if I had gotten tenure when I originally applied . . . I tried not to think of the money being spent on the suite of administrative offices. I tried not to be bitter.

My physician wanted to prescribe Prozac or Paxil. Take your pick, he said.

I panicked.

Perhaps my powers of description had failed me. Perhaps I was being too obtuse, too indirect, too pedagogical with the doctor. I tried again. I told him that I felt fine on the rare weekends I did not go into my office. I told him that even after those weekends, by Thursday I was sick again and weak. I told him I had fevers. I told him again about the vomiting, the fainting, the vertigo.

"Are you depressed?" he asked me.

I didn't cry.

He made the decision for me. Paxil, he said, try Paxil.

My lawyer later told me that I could not sue him because I never filled the prescription.

Only one student came to see me all the times I was in the hospital. She brought directed independent study forms for me to sign. Her project description had something to do with ecolesbianism and Rachel Carson, the author of *Silent Spring*. Now I wish I had paid more attention: to the student's name and to her theory. Then I could only shake my head. I could not even hold the pen to sign my name to the form.

Or maybe the student was a dream.

I am telling Linda about the student's project. Telling her the student had completed the project and that it was brilliant. "It should be published by now," I say. I am suitably proud, although I knowingly but modestly try to imply that the student could never have done it without me.

Linda only says, "I'm in the LPN program."

"This is relevant," I argue.

On a good day, I argue with Linda.

This can be difficult because she does not argue back. I suppose they teach the interns at Helping Hands techniques to avoid conflict. I assume they instruct them not to engage in hostility. We are to be helped, not aggravated. There is no one to whom I could explain that a good argument—an abstract argument about aesthetics, for example—would help me more than having my damn dishes washed.

But sometimes I can get Linda a little riled. If I'm honest, I'll admit it's probably more her mood than any technique of mine. But I have to take credit for even the smallest successes these days.

Like the day I complained to her about the development down the road. I had been driving to the Grand Union, but hadn't felt confident enough to make the turn into the parking lot because my clutch leg was going a bit numb, so I'd just kept driving, then turned up the road thinking I could circle back. That's when I saw it. The hill stripped of trees and dotted with yellow machines. Men in heavy boots dancing around with orange streamers, marking this or that for destruction and construction.

It made me so dizzy with anger that I drove back home without getting any groceries.

I asked Linda about it, trying for a casual tone.

"It's going to be a mall," she explained.

"A mall? A mall? Why do we need another mall? There's one not far from here." I suppressed a memory of an argument with Alexis one summer, at the ice cream store in the climate-controlled cavern called Mountain Mall.

"This one will be bigger. And it's a lot closer."

"What, people can't drive twenty miles to go shopping?" I said snidely, as if I were not a person who could barely manage to drive two miles.

Linda shrugged. "It's been controversial. Haven't you been reading the newspaper?"

"It really makes me angry." Part of my vehemence came from avoiding her question, not wanting to admit that I find the local paper pretty weak. And not wanting to admit that I'm worried that the ink from the paper will have some hidden chemical that will make me sneeze and redden and gasp for oxygen.

"Doesn't tearing up the pristine land to erect some ugly mall make you sick?"

Linda's nostrils flared slightly. "First of all, it used to be a landfill."

"Great! Shopping on top of toxic waste."

"You're just angry because you're sick. Not really because of the mall," Linda said, finally departing from her training as a Helping Hands volunteer.

"What do you think made me sick?" I challenged.

"Not the mall," she answered matter-of-factly. "You were sick before you moved here."

"Maybe not this particular mall, but malls in general. The mall-ness of life."

Linda sighed, her irritation subsiding. "Besides," she added, "it will mean a lot more jobs for people in the community."

I tried to engage her again. "Sure, minimum-wage jobs."

Linda looked at me accusingly. I knew what she was thinking. That I was some city snob come up here for the wilderness, such as it was. That I could afford to preserve the land, what with my disability payments and my summer cottage insulated into a yearlong house. That I was some former professor, head stuck in the clouds, without an inkling of what it took to survive.

"I make more than minimum wage," Linda finally said. It was then I learned that Protection Unlimited had assigned Linda to the construction site. Guarding the steel beams from theft. Guarding the earth movers from being moved. Guarding the enemy.

On a bad day, I can hear the clanging of the machines in the distance. The sound of metal on metal. The sound of the ground groaning in desperation. I can hear the earth screaming inside my own head.

On a good day turned into a bad day, I try to drive to the Grand Union, only to be halted by some huge truck flagged with fluorescent OVERSIZE LOAD banners and surrounded by police cars with flashing lights as if it were a parade instead of a waste of my tax dollars and more destruction.

On a good day, I sit on my deck and read books I have ordered from the Mountain Library system or from on-line bookstores. One book leads me to another. I liked Rachel Carson's letters and I admit I find it reassuring to think of her as a dyke since so much of the other environmental stuff seems to have been written by staunch men with beards and axes. Like all the ecological defense stuff. I can't believe that some of these books aren't illegal. They have instructions on how to spike trees to deter timber sales. And how to forestall roads to impede development of the wilderness. And how to cut fences and disenable snares to save animals. I reread the sections on destroying heavy machinery.

Water and diesel don't mix.

Sand in the oil tank is very effective.

An articulated loader pivots in the center.

Sugar and syrup are overrated.

Introduce abrasives into the lubrication system.

In the local paper, to which I am a new subscriber, I read about a gas blast at the mall construction site. A drilling contractor punctured a gas main, creating a "wall of fire" that damaged eleven vehicles.

There is nothing in the ecology books about creating a gas blast.

"The ninth accident at the job site since June," the newspaper reports.

I try to keep the newspaper as far away from me as possible, but have to raise it closer to my face to read the inset that lists the other accidents: a backhoe ruptures a sewer line; a tractor-trailer spills two hundred gallons of diesel fuel, which flow into storm drains; four water mains break.

There is nothing about spilling fuel or breaking water and sewer lines.

Perhaps there is a different book about ecological activism that I haven't seen.

The afternoon sun slants on the wood slats; the black squirrels, wearing their luxurious mink coats, run around in circles burying this or that.

"You shouldn't be out here in this chill," Linda says when she arrives. She brings a chenille spread out to the chair, arranging it so that the hole in the fine fabric is concealed, and asks me if I want a cup of tea. I agree, closing my eyes against the fact that she is anything other than my considerate lover, home from a hard day.

"How was school?" I ask her, hoping to prolong my fantasy.

"Fine." The answer of a petulant child to a prying adult.

"That good, eh?" I return to my book.

"It's actually pretty bad," Linda admits when she brings me my cup of tea. Lemon Zinger, no sugar and the tea bag removed, just the way I like it. I blow on the tea, making a careful ripple across the surface, waiting for Linda to talk.

When she finally does, she is close to crying. I notice that both of her eyes start to tear at exactly the same time, though not a drop of moisture can escape her eyelids the way she wipes them with the back of her hand. I want to take her in my arms and tell her that everything will be fine, that she has nothing to cry about, but instead I find myself all professorial. Not all that strange, since she is having a student problem. Grades.

"It's stupid," she says. "Or I guess I am."

"No one is stupid," I say, although I've never really believed this. Or never believed that everyone is good at academics, which doesn't mean anything about intelligence. I have always tried to believe this.

"It can't be all that bad." I smile at her.

Because I'm thinking, even if she can't read French, even if she can't read English, at least she can reach the damn saucepan to boil some water to make some tea. So it's hard for me to feel sorry for her. Hard for me not to think I should have the damn stainless-steel whistling kettle that Alexis now has. I don't remember Alexis liking tea. Maybe her new girlfriend does.

I don't remember Linda bringing me the tea. Maybe we sipped together.

I don't remember Linda leaving. But she isn't here now.

I think I remember the stepladder. Or a stool. I'm not sure what I was using, what I was looking for—the saucepan for more tea? the blue box I have not been able to find since I moved? the funnel I know I have and now might need? I only know that I've fallen; only know that I can't move my legs, can't feel them. I only know that now it's dark, but that happens when it's barely five o'clock; I only think that if Linda is gone, she won't be back until tomorrow. But, I hope, I'll be off the kitchen floor by then. I will not be lying on the tiles, my face on the long blue rug that runs the length of the sliding-glass doors. I will be sitting propped up in my chair as if nothing whatsoever has happened.

I have been dreading this. But it isn't as bad as I thought it would be. I'm not panicked, for example. That's what I've always been afraid of, panicking. But I'm relatively calm. There's nothing to do except wait. Wait until Linda comes or my strength comes—whichever comes first. I could think that neither of those things will happen. I could think that Linda will never come back or that my strength will never return, but I don't think those things. Not yet, anyway. I have postponed thinking about them until another nightfall. If the night passes and then a day passes, then I will allow myself such thoughts.

Now, I try to entertain myself with my mind. When I was in college, they were always soliciting student volunteers for sensory deprivation experiments. They would put a student in a dark tank of water, totally suspended in a soundless world, to see how long the student could tolerate an environment without external stimulation. One could push a panic button or something, which many students did after a few minutes, believing they had been in the tank for hours and hours. "It's like the end of the world," one student proclaimed.

The common knowledge around campus was that the

mathematics students could stay in the tank the longest. The secret seemed to be focusing on things that didn't require perceptions. Apparently, the math whizzes recited equations to themselves or something. Liberal arts students were the worst. As an English major, I never volunteered. The only thing I had memorized were some song lyrics, which I didn't think would amuse me very long. My memory has always been bad.

It isn't much better now. As a deconstructionist, I need a text to deconstruct. Who could recall all of *The Well of Loneliness*? Who can even recall the first line? Not me. The only text I have handy is my own life.

This could be my *In Search of Lost Time*, which I still think of as *Remembrance of Things Past*, thanks to the Moncrieff translation. My *A la recherche du temps perdu*. Yes, much better in French. Like everything. Even *cookie* sounds better in French: *madeleine*.

I should never have chosen English.

English is dangerous.

Sure, it seemed like a safe occupation. A literature professor, ensconced in an ivory tower; what could be less hazardous than that? What could happen to me, a paper cut? A little carpal tunnel syndrome? More likely I could be crushed by my own ego. Who would think I would become an environmental-illness casualty? Who would think the university would put the office of the author of *Aesthetics and Argument in Women's Literature* next to the Zoology Lab? Who would know that the main function of the lab was not the study of cute and furry creatures but the destruction of them? Who could have guessed that I was being poisoned, slowly and then not so slowly, by the chemicals wafting through the walls, into my office and into my lungs, and into my blood? My cup of coffee was toxic. And not from the caffeine.

"Nerve damage. Compromised immune system. Abnormal tissue." That's what the lawyer said. My lawyer. The university's lawyers said no such things. During the deposition, the university's lawyer kept asking me about diagnosis and the

results of the tests on my blood and my equilibrium. I kept trying to answer with how I felt ("dizzy," I said; "itchy from
rashes," I said; "like I can't breathe," I said), but the lawyer
told me to state what I knew about the EEG, or the EKG, or the
CT, or the MRI.

"Isn't that hearsay?" I asked, trying for some legal phrase-
ology.

"I ask the questions," he said, "and you answer them."

"I don't know the answers."

"You can just say you don't know," my lawyer instructed
me.

"That's hard," I said, "I'm an English professor. I'm supposed to know the answers."

No one laughed.

"Ask me something about feminine *écriture*," I said.

Everything sounds better in French.

The stenographer asked me how *écriture* was spelled.

"I know the answer to that." I laughed.

Alone.

Paralyzed on the floor, I could let the scent of the Lysol waft
me into my childhood as sturdily as the lemon tea and *madeleine*
carried Marcel Proust. Though Proust wasn't made sick by sniffing; I should switch to something less toxic for cleaning. And
my memory is no match for his. I scurry through my mind,
upturning the leaves that litter my forest floor, and do not find
any of the treasures I so carefully buried. When my mother and
stepfather disowned me when I was twenty-one, I hid their
existence, even from myself.

And in my foraging, even if I do find some meaty nut that I
can crack and consume, I have no idea whether it is mine or
someone else's. I have read and reread other women's lives; I
have criticized the critical commentary; I have deconstructed
author and character. I am not sure I never lived in a room with
yellow wallpaper, or in a house by the gray sea watching the
lighthouse blink, or in Africa. Was it my lover who left me when
I became sick or was that a character in a lesbian romance?

It must have been a character. Real people are not that cruel.

My lawyer told me I did great at the deposition. I thought she must be crazy. I couldn't answer anything they asked me about my condition. And then there was the whole embarrassment before we even got into the conference room.

There were stairs.

A small set, not even a flight, four or five steps at most, separating the large wading pool of the reception area from the busy stream of lawyers who flowed from the tributaries of their offices and eddied in the conference rooms. Four stairs; five at most. Their purpose aesthetic rather than architectural. Or perhaps symbolic. But whatever their reason, they were a hurdle for the wheelchair.

I hadn't wanted to use the wheelchair.

I thought I could walk, leaning on my three-prong cane.

But the day before, I had fallen down the front steps at one of my physician's offices. Why a damn doctor would have an office with steps was a mystery to me. And now I couldn't walk.

My lawyer was raising a fuss.

The university's lawyers were trying to be nonchalant.

Then one of them, not the one who would ask questions during the deposition, but another one, older and bigger, more like a regular guy instead of a lawyer, his hair not as styled, his hands not as smooth, took charge. Enlisting the other lawyers to pick up the wheelchair and its occupant—me—and lift us over this "small problem."

They almost dropped me. A wheelchair is heavier than it looks.

One lawyer clutched his spine, moaning. The older lawyer scolded, "I told you to lift with your knees, not your back."

After the deposition, there was a piece of plywood on the stairs, and I rolled down, half afraid that the wood wouldn't hold the weight, but it did.

"You were really great," my lawyer said.

I figured she meant because I didn't die from humiliation.

Only when I am awakened by the glare of my house's security lights do I realize I must have fallen asleep. That is one thing I always wondered but never asked: why the students in those sensory deprivation experiments simply did not fall asleep.

I would have fallen asleep during some of the medical tests, I convinced myself, if only I hadn't been bothered so often. Especially the MRI. The technicians strap you on a narrow bed and then you slide into a capsule, all snuggly and safe and claustrophobic. I told myself this was my chance at sensory deprivation. But the moment the senses relaxed into emptiness, the clanging started. Followed by a symphony of jackhammers. Then the technician's voice. Breathe this way or that. Hold the breath. Exhale and hold the breath some more. Then more jackhammers. Then voices. Then the taste in the mouth of the metallic fluid from the IV. Then clanging. And on and on for fifty minutes.

Even if I had known some equations, I wouldn't have been able to recite them.

Even if I had been able to sleep, I would have been awakened.

Maybe I am still sleeping now and the huge ghostly rat at the sliding-glass door is a dream. It must be a dream; a real rat, even out here in the country, would not be so large. Or so furry. And a real rat would avoid the security lights shining on the deck. It wouldn't be snuffling with its pink nose and blinking its pink eyes, feeling the wooden deck with its pink fingers.

This albino rodent is looking right at me, though it doesn't seem to see me. Our faces are maybe six inches apart. Luckily the sliding-glass door is thick. And between us.

It is walk-rolling as slow as I do when I'm very tired, though at least I don't have dirty white fur everywhere. Except for the tail. Which looks naked and shaved and as vulnerable as a sex organ. It's waddling around the deck, sniffing, I suppose, for food, prowling casually, its fingers rubbing at a spot on the wood. Finally, it waddles off the deck, into the yard, out past the halo of the security lights.

If I were in the sensory deprivation tank, I would push the button now. Just so I could find out the time. How long have I been immobile here on the kitchen floor. Maybe all those English graduate students were not panicked, just curious. Not apathetic like those mathematics students.

My legs are not cooperating, but I think they feel a little less numb. I try to use my arms to push myself back from the sliding-glass door. If I could turn myself around, maybe I could use my arms to swim myself back to my bedroom.

I know I've really been asleep this time when I wake up again to a sea of beige light. Know I've really been dreaming. Alexis. So fucking unfair. She never appeared in my dreams when I lived with her. But now, she's always popping up. Always kissing my breasts or caressing my thighs.

"In your dreams," she used to say in that sarcastic tone she was always perfecting.

There are two, then three black squirrels on the deck. Smaller than last night's rodent and dark as eggplant. It seems to me as if the dark animals would come out at night and the pale ones would prefer the daylight, but I guess it's the opposite. One has a nut in its mouth. The animal sits on its hind legs, baring its dark stomach, its tail like a pirate flag whipping in the morning breeze. Another squirrel approaches, and the first one scampers away, but not far, until it looks over its squirrel shoulder at its companion. Then the third one runs between the two of them, until there is a circle of black squirrels, chasing one another and stopping to wait for one another and it's hard not to think they are having a damn fine time.

The birds provide the tunes for this sexual squirrel production, here on the dance floor of the deck just past dawn.

The machines from the mall construction clang in the distance.

If I ever manage to get off this damn floor, I am going to remember to feed the squirrels and not just the birds.

If I ever stand up again, I am going to stop the mall. Blow the fucker to bits.

Not if. When. When.

Like a prisoner plotting and planning what I will do when my sentence is over. There must be parole. This cannot be a life sentence without that possibility.

"Degenerative condition," the lawyer said. My lawyer. When I get up off this floor. When. When. I am going to seduce Linda. Or let her seduce me. It's possible. There's some feeling that could turn into action; some confidences exchanged; some mug of tea passed from hand to hand, the fingertips touching a mere moment longer than strictly necessary.

The black squirrels come back to cavort on the deck for a minute, as if to celebrate this idea.

"In your dreams," Alexis would say.

It's like a dream, really. Me pulling myself across the floor. Managing for a while on my knees, my legs almost unnumbed. Crawling the final few feet to the bedroom. Flopping myself into bed. The best part is managing to get my pants off.

It seems as if I've just fallen asleep, my quilt more comforting than any lover, but it's dark again when I hear Linda. She's brought some food, Chinese chicken, I think, but what I really want is for her to help me to the damn bathroom.

I don't tell her I spent the night on the kitchen floor.

I do tell her about the huge furry albino rodent.

"Possum." She laughs.

She's making some tea. I waddle to the couch, my legs feeling almost normal. Normal for me, anyway.

I am wishing I had on those silk aubergine pajamas. But I'm not sure I even know where they are now. Probably with the missing box. Wrapped around the box or inside the box with the letter granting me tenure and an anniversary card from Alexis.

I am looking at Linda's jeans. Faded blue. Baby blue, the moment before the knee is about to rip, revealing clouds of white string.

I am imagining my face on the thigh of that soft, soft fabric, my cheek rubbing against the pulls in the warp of the thin denim.

I am sipping tea.

Linda is crying, serious crying now. Not just gleaming eyes, but wet cheeks and sobs.

It takes me a while to notice this, but when I finally do, at least I put down my tea and stop thinking about her jeans and act like a concerned human being.

It's her paper for her internship: "The Psychology of Disability."

Without an acceptable paper she won't get passing grades for her course, without which she won't get her LPN degree, without which she'll never get a permanent—and paid—position at Helping Hands and she'll be working nights at Protection Unlimited as a security guard for the rest of her life and maybe not even that because the guards are thinking about honoring the picket line of the carpenters' union at the mall construction site.

I am telling her I'll help her.

"Do you have a draft?"

"Just some notes in the car."

"Go get it."

"Right now?"

"I'm not going anywhere." I smile.

I need her departure to digest my new realization. I've lived pretty much my whole life in semesters, the seasons of academia, but now that I don't, I guess I thought such rhythms had ceased to exist. I thought Linda was forever, or at least as forever as anything ever is. I knew that I was her subject, her internship, that she brought me tea for college credit. But I somehow forgot that the arrangement was limited to a semester.

Next semester there would be someone else.

A stranger.

If I'm lucky.

Unless Linda could get a permanent position at Helping Hands and I could be part of her permanent assignment.

It's atrocious. There's no other word that does it justice. She had obviously never absorbed the concept of the topic sentence. Or what came after: the development of an idea. Never mind its deconstruction; it had to be constructed first. This was basic stuff.

I try to figure out a tactic that does not involve me rewriting her paper. But first I blurt out my astonishment that she had gotten out of high school, never mind this far at the community college.

"There weren't many papers. And my lover—my former lover—used to help me." Linda achieves a slight lilt in her voice. "She works for the newspaper now," she adds, as if this explains something.

"Type your notes up on my computer," I tell her, hoping a nice font will make everything look better.

"Sources?" I ask her, looking at her draft.

"It's supposed to be reflective," she says.

I sigh.

"Write more," I say. "Don't stop until you have twenty pages."

"It only has to be fifteen," she complains.

"You'll need twenty," I say.

Obviously the woman has never heard of editing.

We are sitting on the couch, days later, talking about her finished and submitted paper, though I'm thinking again that I might try to find my blue box and those aubergine silk pajamas, when she kisses me. It isn't a chaste kiss. There is some teasing tongue to it.

"Sorry," she says.

"I'm not." I smile.

She guides me to bed like she has done a hundred and one times before, only this time she joins me.

My skin feels scabbed wherever her hand lands; her gentlest touch scrapes against me. It doesn't hurt me, not really, but I imagine how I feel to her: ugly.

"I don't want pity," I say.

"How about a back rub?" she asks.

I demur and she withdraws.

This is the end, I think, cursing myself, but also, I admit, relieved.

But it isn't the end. She is still next to me; we are lying face-to-face on the bed, so close I could count her eyelashes, which I start to do. I keep losing count and my fingers reach up to smooth her cheek, close under her eye socket. Her skin is soft there, though marked with creases and a small bruise where a vein has contorted. It's beautiful, but I don't say that to her.

Instead, my fingers follow the bone until it curves under the fur of her eyebrow, then my fingers slide across to her temple. I make circles there for a while with my index finger, but my pinkie keeps straying into her hair, bringing the other fingers along for the tangle. My thumb becomes enamored of her skull; it seems uniquely solid.

I'm floating. Floating in the sensory deprivation tank of my bed, where it seems she and I have been forever. Maybe only a few seconds have passed; maybe several hours.

I have my mouth on her neck now. I want to suck the hard muscle there. She tastes of sweat, but not unpleasantly.

She reaches for my shoulder; I stiffen involuntarily. She recants.

I have my ear on her chest. I can hear her heart, more of a whoosh than a beat, I think. I try to decipher its messages, listening for a change as my hand brushes against her breast, finding the nipple and almost scratching it. The whoosh is still soft. I rearrange myself so that I can reach her thighs, keeping my ear to the ground of her chest, hoping for a significant rumble. Her heartbeat stays constant as I pull my hand along the bed between her thighs, finding the small stand of her hair, like aspen, I think, though I'm not exactly sure what aspen feels like. Perhaps pines, I revise, pines with curly needles.

I want to linger, but then she exhales suddenly, the hot wind of her breath at the top of my head, and then I'm deep in what I had been imagining as her streams and canyons, only I'm not so certain of my images now, only that I want her. And that I'm as open and unfenced as an undiscovered prairie and she is everywhere all at once.

She doesn't ask me what I like and afterward she doesn't ask me what I had liked or whether I had liked any of it. That isn't the only difference from Alexis, so sure of herself except when something couldn't be calculated, but it's the one that seems most explicit, as I drift off to sleep, feeling Linda's heart whoosh against my back.

Linda starts coming over in the evenings, before she has to leave for the eleven-to-seven shift at Protection Unlimited, guarding the construction site.

On a good evening, we have sex.

On a bad evening, I drink tea and ignore the dizziness that pulses behind my eyes and listen to her tell stories. Her old girlfriend. Her childhood. Her camping trip to Michigan's Upper Peninsula.

Even the bad evenings are good.

She starts coming over in the mornings too, after her shift at Protection Unlimited and before her classes at Mountain Community and Technical College.

On a good morning, I make her breakfast and watch her nap.

On a bad morning, she makes breakfast and we nap together.

One morning, she pulls me close to her and I put my mouth to her neck to kiss my favorite muscled spot there and inhale the smells of her scalp. As I move away, I get dizzy and feel my knees tremble. Then my eyes blur and I start coughing. The next thing I remember, I'm in bed.

"I'll be back," she says.

I wonder if she will be. I wonder if she has gone to join Alexis.

But she comes back, showered and changed. I feel better, although not good enough to eat the toast she brought me.

"Sorry," I apologize. "I don't know what happened." I hate apologizing for not feeling well, but it seems I always apologize anyway.

"It was probably me. The chemicals," she says.

"Chemicals?"

"Yeah. They've been spraying at the construction site."

"Spraying what?"

"Fumigating. You know, the place used to be a landfill."

"So what's left to kill?"

"Rodents, mostly."

I turn away from her, trying not to think of the black squirrels, dead over there at the site of the future mall.

Dead as rats.

Dead as we all would be. Dead as the earth would be. It isn't bad enough they had to tear up the earth, they have to poison everything just to make certain they achieved their ugly purpose.

She gets a B-plus on her paper.

The semester is over.

Neither one of us mentions it.

On a good or a bad evening, after she leaves, I practice trying to see in the dark, like some nocturnal animal, like a possum. Night vision is important. Defending the earth against the machines is best done in the deep of the dark.

I find socks that fit over my shoes: obscures footprints.

I have gloves and a ski mask: both black.

I locate a pot holder that I can tie to the bottom of my three-prong cane: my own idea. The ecodefense books I read in the long afternoons do not seem to anticipate my kind of activist.

There are more newspaper articles about the mall. One written by Linda's former girlfriend, which is pretty weak on topic sentences and paragraphing skills, but seems to imply that the gas explosion might not have been an accident. Perhaps I have co-conspirators somewhere.

There's a strike. The Carpenters Local voted. Wages and working conditions. Some security guards are crossing the line.

"Scabs," I say.

"Double-time," Linda says.

"Selling out," I say.

"Have to eat," Linda says.

"Well, I'm glad you're not doing it." I smile, grateful that Protection Unlimited has transferred Linda to another job, at Mountain Community and Technical College, as a matter of fact. I suggest she spend most of her time guarding the books in the library, but she says that's not possible because she has to make rounds or something, and besides, she's done with her work for her courses.

"You could read Proust." I try to make my recommendation lighthearted but serious.

"Is he one of those save-the-trees people you're always reading?"

"No," I answer. "You might like him."

"I'll try to look him up," she half promises.

We are sliding into other half promises and half plans. We're shaping schedules into habits, into a future. We both hope it will snow on Christmas Eve and think this coincidence so amazing we promise we will spend the night together, here in the cottage that I'm coming to think of as our house. Our house.

Our.

For the holidays, I order Linda a few things. Silk aubergine pajamas from an expensive catalog. And a very abridged, one-volume edition of Proust's *In Search of Lost Time*. And a not-so-abridged edition of *The Well of Loneliness*. I hint that I want a tea kettle.

I am going to cook a Christmas Eve feast. I talked to the manager at Grand Union and ordered a kosher roasting chicken. I'll stuff it with rosemary and lemons; I'll use oysters and bread for dressing; I'll improvise some exotic gravies. It will be better than any Christmas Eve in the French countryside.

We have a small argument; very small. I'm not sure what it's about. It is not about me being too circular and squirrellike, or about her being too sarcastic. I think it has something to do with the tea kettle and the chicken and the oysters.

It ends when Linda yells at me that she doesn't want me for my money.

It hadn't occurred to me that she did, at least until she tells me she doesn't.

And then she says, "Something came up."

She has to go to her parents for Christmas Eve.

I figure this is the end of the semester.

She tells me she could come over on Christmas, later in the day.

I try to act casual.

I don't want the pity of Christmas Day when she had promised Christmas Eve, so I tell her I now have my own plans for Christmas. Not with my own parents, the ones who sent me the usual holiday card, the ones she thinks are dead.

No, I tell her Alexis is coming.

On Christmas Eve.

To spend the night.

She turns away from my lie; I can't see if her eyes glisten with the wetness of regret.

It's true I have plans.

I'm going to the mall on Christmas Eve. Not for last-minute shopping, for at this mall there is nothing to buy. And if I have my way, there never will be.

Sabotage. A French word.

On Christmas Eve, it is not snowing.

I put my funnel and my milk carton of sifted sand in my backpack. I've memorized the locations of oil fillers on backhoes and bulldozers and articulated loaders.

Maybe it isn't any colder than usual, but it feels colder to me. My gloves are on my hands and my socks are over my boots. The ski mask makes me feel like a criminal.

I am stiff.

Dizzy.

I am too ill to go.

No. No. I'm feeling better than I have in months.

I'm strong. I am.

It's just a matter of willpower.

No one ever said I lacked willpower.

Not even Alexis.

But it does seem as if I'm smaller than usual. Scrambling into my truck, I look up through the open door and see a slit of moon I could swear is farther away than it was last week. The roads are pretty empty, it's past dark and past dinner, and most everyone who was going somewhere is already there.

I try to imagine Linda at her parents' house, which is difficult, since I don't know much about their house, even where it is, or what her parents are like. I suppose I should have asked, but I also suppose she should have told me.

Past the Grand Union, closed and dark, I turn my little truck up the hill and then into a small lot, being careful to stay on the paved part. Don't want to leave tire tracks in the dirt. I sidle out of my truck, keeping my cane close, hoping not to have to use it. I slide along in my sock-covered boots, pretending to myself that this is a good way to obscure my footprints rather than necessary to forestall the cane.

The wind batters me. There is little protection out here. There are no trees, none. Once there were so many trees in this part of the world that squirrels could travel for miles going limb to limb and never touch the ground. At least according to the books.

Sand should be sifted for the best abrasive effect on the engines.

At least according to the books.

The big machines, sleeping on Christmas Eve, are farther away than they seemed; farther away than the moon. Or I am weak, getting weaker. The backpack, with its funnel and the milk carton of sifted sand, beats against my back.

My breath stings my own lungs.

My fingers are numb in my gloves.

My cane dangles.

I look back, grateful for my night vision, perfected and practiced. But I'm worried to see that the truck is just as far away behind me as the big machines are in front of me. I am out here in the middle of the sensory deprivation tank of the entire universe, unsure how long it has taken me to get this far, certain it will take me longer to get back. I must go on. The fate of the earth is at stake.

Use a funnel to pour the sand into the oil.

According to the books.

"Didn't you think it was strange that you were the only one down there?" she asked.

Alexis.

The university neither admits nor denies that the activities in the Small Mammal Research Development Office or the Zoology Laboratory caused the plaintiff to become ill.

Settlement Agreement.

I hear something. Some sound. Some rustling. Must be the rats, I think. No. No, it's probably a possum. Better yet, some black squirrels, staying up tonight to accompany me.

I feel dizzy.

I'll just rest a bit. Shift my backpack. Steady myself with my pot-holdered cane. Adjust my eyes.

Acid. That's my first thought.

Then I realize it's just light. A flashlight, huge as the sun, bitter bright and full in my face. The universe is obliterated.

I'm caught, I realize.

I'll never confess, I promise.

I hear my name.

I hear a soft sigh, a muffled laugh, a rush of words.

"How did you know?" she murmurs as she pulls me close.

"Triple-time," she starts.

"Your old girlfriend?" she asks.

I lean against her, my eyes and ego stinging. I bury my face in her neck, trying to find that muscled part, deep beneath her jacket. Trying to smell her scalp. Trying to hear the whoosh of her heart.

Maybe she's my co-conspirator. Maybe she's here to sabotage.

It's my momentary desire.

A poisoned corpse under her circling words. She's here to work. To guard. To make extra money.

She's sorry she lied.

She wanted to buy me a present.

And how did I know?

And what am I doing here?

If only my backpack boasted a rosemary-and-lemon-filled chicken with tender but crisp skin. Instead of sand and a funnel.

I will think of a way to explain this.

I will.

My left eye squints open, hoping to meet her eyes, but my field of vision is filled with the collar of her Protection Unlimited uniform, an absolutely resplendent green.

The Death of the Subject

"not only is the bourgeois individual subject a thing of the past, it is also a myth; it never really existed . . ."

—*Fredric Jameson*
in **Postmodernism and Its Discontents**

"Useless, there is no god of healing in this story."

—*Cassandra*
in **Oresteia** by *Aeschylus*

The smell and sound of the sea. The taste of salt. The feel of my skin stiffening from too much sun.

I crave sensations that are not anchored by the albatross of the visual.

Certainly I am grateful for my sense of sight. That's how I earn my living and it is a comfortable one in the scheme of things. But like all work, mine has its own peculiar curse. Relentlessness. I never have a day off, never a night of relaxation. Not just because my girlfriend, Agnes, is a detective with the police department and is always cajoling me for clues.

The curse of her own work, I suppose. But even curled next to Agnes after some sweaty sex, listening to her breathy contentment, I am on duty. I can close my eyes, but I cannot escape. I'm a seer. A see-er. They call me the fortune-teller of Surf Palace. My rates are considered reasonable. My predictions are considered accurate.

You can believe whatever you desire; people always do.

Another sort of curse, I suppose.

Their curse, not mine.

I do not believe in belief.

Desire, of course, is another story. Everyone's story. Even if I did not have my visions to assist me, I could work the tourist trade at Surf Palace. All people expect is a hand sparkling with a few silver rings and some sympathy toward their thwarted desires. A little hope is a bonus.

My client, as almost always, is a woman.

I take her fingers in mine. I point to the array of tarot decks and instruct her to select one. The round women's cards. The Knight-Rider deck. The Native-American medicine cards. The PoMo tarot. She never picks PoMo—the postmodern deck alienates her with its images of televisions and Elvis Presleys, although it is my favorite. She finds it too familiar, too mundane. She doesn't realize that it doesn't matter. The cards are a ruse. I watch her as she shuffles the cards, but what I see is a Technicolor pastiche.

Her struggle is happiness.

My struggle is articulation—the translation of pictures into language. It is as if I am a foreigner who understands what is being said but cannot make herself heard. It makes me envy the psychics who hear voices and need only repeat the words with cautious and important tones. I can only hope for a word or two to appear among the shifting shapes, a piece of text pasted on the messy collage that zips through my mind.

My struggle is isolation—the segregation of information. My perception is a conglomeration, a chorus of pop art derived from a million sources. Which fragment from this animated junkyard will touch her heart? As if there is only a single segment, as if she is not as assorted as my kaleidoscope. Like everyone else, she thinks she is so special, so unique, such an individual.

I will tell her she is so different, so wonderful, such a good lover—if I decide to touch more than her fingers. If I kiss her. If I lick her breast, lightly with a flicker, before becoming more serious.

I will not tell her what happens. How the images become almost unbearably intense. How the video brightens and sharpens and achieves a speed faster than comprehension. How her life passes behind my eyes as if she is falling from Thrasher's French Fries, the highest building on Surf Avenue, atop which the time and temperature pulsate in blood-colored digits. I will not tell her this: At the moment of her orgasm I see her last moment. She is old or she is not; she is in a car crash or in a hospital bed; she is sliding into the darkness or she is fighting. She is, but she will not always be.

I will not tell Agnes about her, *any* her. My girlfriend, the detective, is the jealous sort. Possessive. "Love is singular," she says. She acts like a charter member of the monogamy society. Except when it comes to her former lovers, especially Clementine, who seems more lover than former most of the time. It's a false intimacy, certainly, or so I tell Agnes, who does not believe me. Agnes tells me I am jealous.

But jealousy cannot account for my visions. No translation, no isolation is necessary: They fuck in my head whenever Agnes is late for a date with me. Clementine is always on top and quite passionate in a vicious sort of way. What I cannot see is whether this is reality or simply Clementine's projections.

My clients are my retribution for Clementine. Or perhaps being physical with some of my women clients is simply another aspect of my occupation. The boundaries between mind and body are obsolete, aren't they?

Once in a while, I meet a woman who actually does seem different, a bit wonderful, and not half bad as a lover. What sets her apart from the others is that she is not entirely self-absorbed; that she is not always looking at me to figure out what I see about her and her meager little life. Though too often even a woman who does not seem self-centered starts asking me questions as if she is interviewing me for a role in the movie she mistakes for her life. "Have you lived in this resort a long time?" "And when did you become a—ah, um, oh—a fortune-teller?" "Is your name really Cassandra?"

I parcel out fragments from my autobiography. Possessing a name such as Cassandra, I explain, tends to limit one's occupational opportunities. Excluding dentistry, for example. She always laughs at this and usually licks her teeth. Also excluding architecture and social work. Hotel/motel management, hairstyling, and waitressing are more plausible, but ultimately unsatisfactory. The only truly suitable occupations for someone named Cassandra, I tell her as she nods her head, are exotic dancing and fortune-telling. There are certainly similarities between the professions, but in the contest between being called a stripper or an oracle, I had no choice but to choose oracle. I have lopsided hips, a congenital condition that prompted several childhood operations, all of them painfully unsuccessful.

I weave my strands into a falsely coherent narrative. I tell her that it was during one of my long recoveries that I started having visions. I thought they were dreams at first, although they did not feel like I was dreaming them. Rather, they felt as if I was participating in someone else's dreams. I knew what my mother had dreamed about me, and not knowing that I shouldn't know something like that, I would talk to her sometimes about the dreams, recalling them as if they were not her dreams at all, but something we had experienced. She was obviously a little confused at first. I suppose she thought that perhaps her own dreams were not dreams after all. And her dreams about me were of the most obvious sort. I was her child, after all, and I was suffering through surgeries because of my misshapen pelvis. She was contorted with guilt. For there had to be some explanation and she was the most likely suspect. That glass of gin? Those cigarettes? Or most probably, some overathletic sexual position.

My client-lover will then steal a glance at my crotch, which she had thought was perfectly normal, and perhaps even normally perfect. Now—coincidentally enough—it does look as if it tilts to the left. Or the right.

When she leaves, she thinks she knows me. I become a story she will tell to her future lovers, always carefully considering whether or not to include the portion about the asymmetrical pelvis. And once in a while, when she has had some wine, she'll embellish it for a few of her friends. Perhaps she will even guess at some of the details I omit. That the images crowding my head made me crazy throughout my adolescence, until MTV went on the air and I understood my visions as music videos without the music. That I'm terrified of doing drugs and will not even swallow a white dot of ibuprofen. That I majored in classics in college and even went to graduate school and started a thesis on postmodern parodies of Greek tragedies. That my mother and I no longer speak, although I know she is now a feminist therapist practicing in Aspen. Or maybe she does not guess at such details; maybe she is not even interested in them.

Even Agnes does not guess, is not interested.

Agnes is only interested in solving her crimes. This newest one is a bit of fag bashing on Surf Avenue. Blood and a baseball bat, stitches and no suspects. No one has been murdered, but Agnes is taking it personally, of course, and has gotten herself assigned to the case even though there is no homicide. At least not yet. Agnes is as serious about her lesbianism as she is about her police work.

Clementine is organizing a protest and advocating that we arm ourselves against the marauders who would destroy our queer-positive resort. Clementine prides herself on her politics as well as her aggressive sexuality. She vociferously proclaims to me that she is not sufficiently appreciated for either: "Even by Agnes," she adds for effect. This usually leads to her harangue about Agnes's job having "killed" Agnes's dyke politics. I'm more interested in the part about "agressive sexuality," but I also hope she doesn't elaborate on that. I think I've already seen more than enough.

I am sitting in Surf Palace, shuffling the PoMo tarot, waiting for a client on this hot and humid summer afternoon. My silver rings swell around my fingers. I turn over a card and then another, inspecting my own fortunes. The suit of guns dominates. It would be gentler in the women's deck (wands) and more medieval in the Knight-Rider deck (swords), but I suppose the message would be the same and that message is not good. But we make our own fates, don't we? I can choose from all the illustrations that crowd my consciousness; I can select the discourse that will construct my life. Representation equals reality. All prophecies are self-fulfilling.

I am surrounded by slogans: "Divers Do It Deeper." "Save the Whales." "Shop Until You Drop." "Visualize World Peace."

I am surrounded by airbrushed animals: Every breed of dog and cat. Endangered species of the rain forest. Marine mammals, including manatees.

I am surrounded by portraits: Trucks. Motorcycles. Rock stars, preferably dead. "Kurt Cobain died for your sins." The silk screen is of the lead singer of Nirvana holding a gun to his head. Suicide commercialized.

I am in a tee shirt shop. Or if not me, at least my perceptions.

There are at least a dozen such shops on Surf Avenue. I never walk through their thresholds; I do not need to. Their window displays reach out and harass me as I pass, walking to the bank, the post office, Surf Palace, or to meet Agnes. And now, the store surrounds me in my reverie. The suit of guns is on the table in front of me, but I am whirling through my visions. It isn't a trance, it's just a different way of seeing. Until I can't see at all. A sudden blackness. A blindness. This has never happened to me before. And it keeps happening. Every time I see all these tee shirts, my seeing soon stops. Making me more nervous than the suit of guns.

What if I lose my second sense of sight? I could continue my occupation, certainly; I could join the ranks of the charlatans. Become more of a therapist, taking after my mother. Agnes would probably leave me because I wouldn't be able to help her solve her crimes. But I could get another girlfriend, couldn't I? I would still be me, wouldn't I? Just a different me, a person not cursed with the video version of the gift of prophecy. I could close my eyes and it would be dark; I'm sure it wouldn't be so frightening after a while. I could kiss a woman and stay inside myself; I'm sure it would be quite enjoyable.

It's really passé to have an identity crisis, Clementine would say. She is flashing through my sanity wearing a tee shirt that declares, "Hate Is Not a Family Value." We are standing on Surf Avenue and the lights pierce the night, carousing around her as if she is the most popular dyke in this summer's trendiest club. Above her, the neon time and temperature sign flashes, framed by the Thrasher's French Fries logo. It is seventy-five degrees. Temperature is very important in a resort town; the vacationers dote on it. It is eleven fifty-nine. Time is illusory; we all pretend it does not matter as the season clicks toward its conclusion.

"This PoMo tarot has got to go," I say. No one is here to hear me, but it does seem to clear the air. I breathe deeply. I smell my own sweat. I should just close my curtains. Take a walk next to the ocean. Rid myself of these visions. Dive under water and swallow some salt water.

I should not just sit here and wait for a client all afternoon. Although I'm not really waiting for a client, I'm waiting for Agnes. She was supposed to stop by and bring me some french fries. She always nags me about eating the fries; says Thrasher's are little bullets clogging each of my arteries; says Thrasher's only changes the oil on Memorial Day and Labor Day; says the cholesterol will kill me. She doesn't know that I won't be dying in any hospital bed. She doesn't know that she won't be either. "Relax and have a few french fries," I want to tell her, but I never do.

Agnes doesn't show up until late afternoon, just as my business is picking up. She is wearing white shorts and a hot-pink tee shirt, the kind without any slogans or pictures on it. She wants to go boating, believe it or not. "A sunset cruise, just the two of us. I've borrowed a little sunfish."

"It does sound romantic," I concede, "but I've got to work."

She sighs. She doesn't really believe that telling fortunes at the Surf Palace is work, unlike chasing murderers.

"What if I told you that this would be work?"

"A workout?" I laugh, planning to act more like I visualize Clementine as being. I reach for her ass.

"No, real work. Like snagging the fag basher."

"On a boat?"

"At the pier."

"What, we're not going to take the Sunfish into the water?"

"No, we will. But we'll also be decoys."

"Decoys? For a fag basher?"

"Don't worry. We'll have backup." She misconstrues my concern. "Some undercovers will be positioned around the pier. We'll be perfectly safe."

"But it doesn't make sense." I wave my hands as if to explain that we are lesbians, which might not necessarily be appropriate bait.

"If you don't want to, I'll understand." Agnes looks at me and I can see the image of Clementine behind her eyes. I think that this means that she will ask Clementine to go if I decline. So I agree.

At the pier, Agnes is holding my hand and kissing me every five seconds. I think that she is happy that we are going boating, until I recall that she is trying to attract the attention of a homophobe. It makes me a little crabby.

Out on the ocean, I'm in a better mood. The dolphins are dancing to the sunset. Surf Palace, the suit of guns, and the sudden darkness all seem very far away. I'm relaxing so much that even the images whirling in my head are soothing, rocking me gently like a tide. Agnes opens a bottle of wine. I feel like a pampered mistress.

"So, can you describe the basher?" Agnes asks.

"No," I answer honestly.

"Are you losing your powers?" she teases.

"No."

"Then what's wrong? Too many pictures?"

"No."

"Too few?"

"None."

"None?"

"I can only see the victim."

"Are you sure it's him?"

"The red-haired one with less freckles than I'd expect, right? The one you introduced me to?"

"That's the one. But is he alone?"

"Not exactly."

"Then?"

"I'm not sure I want to tell you. I know what you'll say."

"I won't say a thing. I promise."

"With Clementine."

Agnes smiles. "You just need to adjust the time frame, darling. Clementine was the first one on the scene. She's the one who dialed 911. She just happened to be there. She's friends with the shop owner and has been checking on the place after closing because he is taking care of his sick lover."

"What a Girl Scout."

Agnes frowns at me.

"That was a lot of blood for such a small cut, don't you think?"

"He was lucky. Clementine found him and scared off the basher. She took him in the store and cleaned him up and bandaged him."

I close my eyes and see Clementine and the victim. She is pouring blood on him. Some from her own menstruation and some from a piece of butchered meat. He is laughing. They are kissing. They are fucking. This time, Clementine is not on top.

"Isn't he the head of some antiviolence thing?"

"Yes, but what are you saying, Cassandra?"

"I'm saying what I'm saying."

"You've never liked Clementine."

"What's to like?"

"I can't believe you. You're letting your personal feelings interfere with the investigation of a crime. You aren't being objective."

"Objective? I don't really assist you by being a paragon of rationality, now do I?" I feel snotty and want her to know it.

"But you are implying—are you not?—that there is something fishy about it."

"Hey, you said it, Ms. Detective."

"Let's go back," she says, sharp enough to let me know that it is not simply a suggestion.

She navigates us back toward the pier. The shore gleams like an ancient island, beautifully raw. It has been almost-dark for a while; twilight lingers in summer. The sky is seared with lavender.

I can almost see the Thrasher's French Fries building. I can see a tee shirt shop. I can see Clementine waiting for us, near Surf Palace. I can see the suit of guns, cards tumbling across Ocean Avenue. I can see Agnes. She is falling. I can't see. That darkness again, complete and so solemn.

"Let's go for a walk down Surf Avenue." Agnes is solicitous again once we are on shore and the boat is bedded. She takes my hand for the benefit of the basher. I look around for someone who looks undercover, but I'm not sure I can trust my own perceptions.

"I am going blind."

"Don't be dramatic, Cassandra." Agnes is annoyed, but she keeps holding my hand. How did I expect her to be sympathetic? I am a captive princess to my prophecies, a seer, a woman with a gift of a goddess. And she is a damn cop. I'm not sure how we ever got together.

The temperature is seventy-nine degrees.

"I'd like some french fries," I tell her.

"You should think of your arteries."

"I'm not going to die from my arteries."

"You think you know everything."

"And you aren't either," I add, just to be mean. "You should have a few fries. They won't make a difference. Clean arteries aren't going to prevent you from dying a violent death. That's your fate, you know."

"Oh, the soothsayer speaketh her amazing prediction! I mean, I am a police officer, after all, so I'd say the odds are pretty good."

"Then why not have a few fucking french fries?"

"Because no bet is a sure bet."

"People believe what they want to believe."

"They sure do," she smiles sarcastically, "even you, Cassandra."

Clementine is the last person I want to see, but there she is, standing outside Sea Shore Tee Shirts. Her own shirt reads, "Hate Is Not a Family Value." I blink my eyes against her. I am filled with desire. For the life that is slipping from me. I want to be back in Surf Palace, shuffling the PoMo tarot, or better yet, shuffling the women's deck, those round cards shimmering like gold in my hands. I could touch the fingers of a client. Touch her hair, which would also shimmer like sunlight against my tan hands.

I am in a restaurant with Clementine and Agnes. Not sure how I got here. They are eating meat. I am having pasta. They are talking, laughing. I am silent. They are drinking. Gin and tonics, I think. I am quiet. I am watching the last few hours skulk by.

We are on the street again. Surf Avenue. We walk past the bank, past the post office. We are outside of Sea Shore Tee Shirts. Clementine is giddy, rude and loud. The streetlights flirt with her. The shops are closed. It is dark but the Thrasher's temperature sign flashes its red proclamation: seventy-five degrees. The Thrasher's time is eleven fifty-one.

Clementine opens a door with a key. "I just have to check something," she says. I can smell french fries, the grease so seductive. I linger at the threshold, but then follow Agnes into the shop.

I am surrounded by slogans: "Divers Do It deeper." "Save

the Whales." "Shop Until You Drop." "Visualize World Peace."

I am surrounded by airbrushed animals: Every breed of dog and cat. Endangered species of the rain forest. Marine mammals, including manatees.

I am surrounded by portraits: Trucks. Motorcycles. Rock stars, preferably dead. "Kurt Cobain died for your sins." The silk screen is of the lead singer of Nirvana holding a gun to his head.

I am surrounded. By Clementine. By Agnes. By that man with the red hair and not enough freckles.

I sense the gun. Not the gun that Agnes carries. Not the gun from the PoMo tarot suit. But the gun that I have seen over and over and over. The gun that I cannot see because it is at the back of my head. What I can see is the Thrasher's French Fries neon time reflected through the windows. Eleven fifty-eight.

"You are such a slut," Clementine hisses at me.

I see a glint, a shimmer. It is not gold.

I am dead, I think. But it is Agnes who crumples. Blood oozes onto the cement floor under her. It is my blood, it is her blood. The distance between us is invisible now. The remnants of all the stories arrange themselves into understanding. It is a sorrow. It is treachery. It is unbelievable, acceptable only because I do not believe in belief. Clementine is a killer who fancies herself a hero. She will possess individual glory as a champion of the cause. She desires, what? Fame? Or something less complex? It will never belong to her, I curse her. And what I see—without the benefit of a curse—is that she too will be covered in an ugly spurt of red.

"Mark my words, Clementine, this will be avenged. You will die a death more brutal than you can imagine."

"You are such a fraud," she says.

"Hurry up and pull the trigger," he says.

There is no final image. Only

re•view

[ri•vyōō´]

v. to look at again
n. a critical discussion of someone's work

A clump of dog hair clung to Marlais's face, but at times like this her Siberian Husky could have been sitting on her head and she would not have noticed. All her attention was sucked into the computer screen, which reflected the brilliance of her words back at her, like a mirror in a fairy tale in which she was the princess-in-disguise who would surely prevail over the evil queen.

And even if it wasn't the groundbreaking words of her own novel shimmering on the screen, this was almost as important. It was a review of someone else's novel. And not just someone else, but a pretty important someone else. Someone who had been called the "best writer of her generation." Marlais didn't yet realize that such an appellation was applied to almost every writer, in one review or another, at some time or another.

"A literary luminary," Marlais typed. Marlais loved alliteration. She was a writer, after all. She loved the sounds of words as well as their meanings. She could hear words in her head, not in her own voice, but in a voice much more sophisticated and smoky than her own. Her inner voice; not the voice she heard leaving the message that she was not at home when she really was, like now, sitting at the computer, having the discipline not to allow anyone to disturb her work.

That's what makes a real writer, Marlais thought to herself. Someone who writes. Someone who writes even when there is a message on the answering machine. A message from her friend Pat, suggesting they meet for coffee. Not a message from some head of some university press saying that she should call immediately because her poetry chapbook had stunned everyone with its beauty and they wanted to publish her immediately. Not a message from an editor at some New York publisher, saying he had heard about her work and wanted to see whatever she had finished on her novel. Not a message about a genius award the foundation would be honored if she would accept. But still, a message.

Though she didn't think she could join Pat for coffee. She had to finish this review and get back to her own novel, which was waiting for her in a rattan manuscript box, a gift to herself last Christmas. She had hinted around to her friends and even to her parents that she wanted one. The only reaction from her father had been something predictable about getting a real job before she turned thirty and saving the money that her aunt had left her for when she "really needed it." She had even stopped and shown the rattan letter box to Pat as they walked past the store windows. Pat had snuffed at the price, saying that the store had a lot of nerve to charge that much for "a bunch of straw." Marlais had hoped the box would go on sale after the holidays, but when it hadn't, she bought it for herself anyway. Of course, she hadn't shown it to Pat.

Sometimes, Marlais thought, one just had to realize the limits of friendship, and even love. Still, in some ways Marlais just couldn't understand Pat. It wasn't as if Pat wasn't a writer, too. They had met, in fact, in a creative writing class in college.

But Pat didn't seem to care about what pen containing what ink she was using; she didn't seem to like smooth paper or colorful stamps or velvet-covered notebooks. Marlais loved all of these things. Though she had to admit, more and more she only used her computer, so none of it seemed to matter. Not even the choices she made about fonts and desktop icons on her screen. Who saw them anyway? Sure, she had to print out her poems and her manuscript, but it seemed most of what she wrote got submitted on e-mail, so that the editors didn't need to retype anything. Including this review.

"Cardboard characters," Marlais typed. Too clichéd? Perhaps. Yes, especially for *The Salon*. This was no punky zine or college rag. This was literary. It was prestigious. All the writers read it. Even the stuck-up types teaching at MFA programs read it. In fact, it was one of her former creative writing professors from college who had recommended her for this gig. This was her first piece for *The Salon* and she knew it had to be good. She hoped it would lead to a few more reviews, but also to some of her own creative work appearing in its pages. Her next project, she promised herself, would be to try to excerpt a portion of her novel into a short story for *The Salon*.

She backspaced her phrase away. But then retyped it. Of course it was a cliché, but everyone who read *The Salon* would know that. She could play with their expectations. Take the cliché and extend it into a metaphor. "Corrugated love scenes," she typed. "Cheap gray landscapes," she typed. Later, she thought, she could string these together into a witty paragraph.

Later, after she walked Anna Karenina, her dog.

And called Pat.

And had coffee. Espresso, which would make her think better.

Marlais's review in *The Salon* appeared on the third page. The first real page of reviews, after the table of contents and the editor's introduction. This was an accomplishment, Marlais knew, which might even be attributable—at least in part—to the wittiness of her review. It was accompanied by a photograph of Constance Berg, the author. The same photo that appeared on the inside back flap of the book. Marlais didn't think it was a very good snapshot. It made Berg look a little bereft and not sexy at all. Like she was trying to smile but somehow couldn't manage it. Marlais would have a very different photo on her own book jacket, she knew. She would look serious and yet sensuous. She would be striking, a flash of the silver ring on her hand nestled at her neckline.

Third page! First review! Marlais telephoned Pat, suggesting coffee. Trying not to tell her about the piece, hoping Pat hadn't yet seen a copy, assuming that the contributor's copy would be mailed before the regular subscription list.

Then she read her published review, looking for typographical errors.

She leafed through the rest of the pages, measuring her review against the others: It was longer or at least as long, not counting the space the author's photo occupied. She read the contributors notes, comparing her statement with the others: It was not as impressive, which was a positive, not a negative, she decided, because it meant she was in good company.

She skipped over the obligatory piece of fiction because she didn't recognize the author's name and skimmed the poems because the names of those authors were more familiar.

Then she read her review.

Again.

And again.

It *was* witty. It sounded good. She could admit to herself now that she had been half afraid of sounding stupid; could admit that she had been visited one night by a sweaty anxiety; could laugh that she had worried that the phrases that had glimmered on her screen would fall flat on the pages of *The Salon*. But that hadn't happened. It was smart. Yes, very smart.

Though when Pat read it at the coffee shop they both called a café, squinting her eyes while Marlais analyzed Pat's face for reactions, Pat had been tepid.

"Don't you think it sounds smart?" Marlais prompted.

"Yeah. Yeah, it does," Pat admitted.

"But not smart enough?"

"No. No, it's smart enough." Pat's voice betrayed her awkwardness.

"Then, what?"

"Maybe too smart."

"There's no such animal," Marlais protested.

"I guess not." Pat sighed.

"So, what's the real problem?" Impatient, Marlais lit a cigarette.

"Ultimately as compelling as an empty box of chocolates?" Pat read from the review, turning a solid statement into a question with her lilt.

Marlais sighed at the effort of having to connect the dots from cardboard to corrugated to empty box so that Pat could see the picture.

But Pat cut short her explanation. "I see that, Marlais, but the whole thing just seems . . . well, sort of . . . well, it sounds mean."

Marlais ordered another espresso.

The conclusion that Pat was envious seeped into Marlais during the night and surfaced by the next morning. And like a strong cup of coffee, it stimulated her. It made her focused and confident. It made her determined.

She turned on her answering machine and took her novel manuscript from its beautifully golden box and turned on her computer. She took her retractable-point Namiki fountain pen from her desk drawer and checked its ink cartridge to forestall the possibility that her words would become invisible at a crucial moment. She selected a small notebook with real wildflowers pressed into its handmade paper cover.

And she wrote.

Sometimes in the notebook and sometimes on the keyboard and sometimes in her head as she made herself another cup of coffee.

Words were everywhere in her apartment and it seemed as if all she had to do was breathe them in and they would be exhaled into sentences and then paragraphs and pages as precious as pure oxygen.

The messages collected on the answering machine: an invitation from Pat for coffee; a recitation of an advertisement for an "employment opportunity" from her father; another call from Pat.

The pages gathered on her desk, floating out of the printer connected to her computer, stacking in the rattan manuscript box. They were good, Marlais thought, even when she reread them.

Outside, the weather changed and changed back again. She noticed it when she walked Anna Karenina. Though mostly she thought about what she was going to write when she finished her chore. Walking the dog, she felt as if whole sentences came down from the sky, not like rain exactly, because rain wets everyone, but more like some arrangement of light one could only see by being in the right place. Wherever Marlais was, she felt as if she was in the right place.

The sky was black as eggplant. The sentence danced in her mind. It hadn't been evening, but she had passed the grocery store with its vegetables in displays that encroached upon the sidewalk. Usually, she hurried past, worried that Anna Karenina would defecate there, witnessed by people who were pushing their thumbs into avocados to determine ripeness. But now, she lingered, letting the dog sniff at the curb, and the line about the sky seemed to rise off the eggplants. She could almost hear them whisper to her: "We are black as night."

The days bled into one another. Night lost its boundaries. Work was the only universe. It was as if she were in love, consumed and consuming, wanting only to lick the sweat from some particular spot of her beloved's neck. It had been like that with Pat, at least at first. When they were in college. Hiding from Pat's roommates, sequestered in Pat's bed with its scrolled iron frame.

Like lust, like love, after a while Marlais's devotion to her manuscript was subjected to the demands of the day. Although some days she did not get dressed until she had to walk the dog, a task which became later and later in the afternoon until Anna Karenina resorted to sitting at the door and whining. She telephoned her father. She paid her rent and telephone bill. She started to collect her mail and to listen to the radio.

She decided on a schedule. Mornings, she seemed to be at her most creative, so she decided to discipline herself not to work in the evenings. She knew she needed to pace herself: The novel was like a marathon, or a semester of Shakespeare. So she met Pat for coffee and occasionally joined her for a dinner that led to wine that led to bed. If she stayed home alone, she watched the television news or read magazines (she eschewed novels, not wanting to be influenced). Sometimes she reread what she had written that day. Or reread her manuscript from the beginning. Or made notes about what she would write the next day.

Sometimes she wrote letters. Letters to people she never wrote to: the former professor who had encouraged her and had recommended her to *The Salon;* a fellow student she had never really liked but who had written her once or twice; her freshman roommate in the ugly dorm room; even one of her aunts, the one who now lived in Melbourne, Australia, teaching some sort of science at the university there. And even in her letters, her words cascaded, forming themselves in chatty, witty pools of clarity.

The mailbox began to reward her. The first of her correspondents to write back was the woman she had known in college who had written her before. The letter was sort of boring, being an account mostly of a day in her life, at her job as a speech therapist, and it was full of phonetic symbols that Marlais skipped over. Marlais received another letter from the speech therapist, before receiving a letter from anyone else, describing another day, but it seemed to Marlais that this letter was the same as the previous one. How terrible to have all one's days the same, Marlais thought.

Mondays seemed to be especially fertile mail days. And this

Monday there was a letter from her former professor, from her aunt, and the new issue of *The Salon*. Marlais hurried the dog on its walk so she could return to her apartment, make herself a strong cup of coffee, and sit at her table with her mail.

Of course, she looked at the magazine first. The cover of *The Salon* was dominated by a photo of Constance Berg, the author whose book Marlais had reviewed in the last issue. Letters! She smiled with the certainty that her review had sparked letters and commentary. Marlais's smile curled back into itself when she started to read the text. *In Memoriam*, the words read.

Constance Berg—who had once been called the best writer of her generation—was dead at forty-eight. The article quickly reviewed her career: an early prize, a novel turned into a made-for-television movie, thirteen books. The article judged her: a "writer's writer," who had garnered critical acclaim but never popular success. The article claimed her: She was a loyal subscriber and reader of *The Salon*. The article concluded: apparent suicide.

Marlais couldn't stop herself from speculating about the method of suicide. Gun in the mouth? No, only male writers of short stories did that. An overdose of sedatives? That was for poets and cowards. An addict's overfilled needle? No one labeled that suicide. Hanging? She was no faggot or Antigone. Drowning? No Virginia Woolf. Head in the oven? And certainly no Sylvia Plath. Slit her wrists? Maybe, maybe, but so messy.

Jump?

Marlais, ten years old, her legs crossed at the ankle although that made her knee socks pull down. Marlais, at the dinner table, her fork held correctly and poised in the eggplant and tomato stew that her father called ratatouille. Her father talking about a man he worked with, another accountant, who had walked up to the roof of their office building and had simply stepped off it, wearing his jacket and tie and carrying his briefcase. Marlais recalled her father shaking his head and laughing, her mother's horrified gasp, and her own desire to crawl under the smooth quilt of her bed and vomit the blood-colored meal.

She telephoned Pat. Left a message. Poured her cold coffee down the sink. Telephoned Pat again.

Tried to write.

Walked the dog.

Tried to write.

Watched television.

Walked the dog.

Read her manuscript.

Telephoned Pat.

Tried to write.

Watched it get dark.

Listened to her own voice, scratchy and ugly, on the answering machine. Listened to Pat's voice asking her if everything was all right, reminding her that Pat had to work at the bookstore late today, telling her to call her back, telling her she loved her.

Went to sleep.

Woke up. Woke up in the eggplant-colored night seeing Constance Berg—or more precisely, a photograph of Constance Berg—jumping off the roof of Pat's apartment building. Must have been a dream, Marlais consoled herself. Too much coffee, Marlais scolded herself.

At the first light, Marlais went to take a hot shower, even before putting the coffeepot on. The author was there, folded in the bathtub, her black-and-white image bent and bleeding gray blood from the graceful wounds in her wrists. Marlais blinked the image away.

She tried to write.

She walked Anna Karenina, avoiding the street with the grocery store, sure that the Siberian husky would shit and sure that the vegetables would look soggy and spoiled. She detoured to the open spaces near the water, but at the river, Marlais saw someone who looked a lot like the best writer of her generation walking along the banks, looking longingly at the current.

She tried to sleep.

She woke up in the afternoon, angry. That author had thirteen books. Critically acclaimed. But even if they were shit, thirteen books were thirteen books. Nothing to kill yourself over. Marlais wanted one book—just one—and then she knew she would have mastered the struggle to be happy. One book, was that too much to ask? Meanwhile, the author who had killed herself had thirteen reasons to live. Thirteen.

At forty-eight, Constance Berg had just published her thirteenth novel. Marlais had toyed with the idea of using that fact in her review, playing off its symbolism as unlucky. But Marlais had abandoned the idea because she knew that the number thirteen also had pagan connections to good things and didn't want to have her point backfire. Besides, she had decided that it was not a good idea to clutter up her review with too many metaphors. The number detail might deflect from the cardboard metaphors, which worked so well. Though Pat hadn't thought so.

Oh shit, Marlais moaned.

Pat. Pat. Jesus Christ, Pat.

"Meet me for coffee," Marlais screamed into the telephone. "I need to talk to you. Pat? Are you there, Pat? Pick up. Something awful has happened."

Marlais's voice became more and more grating, but she screamed into the telephone until Pat's message machine cut her off. Anna Karenina was whining at the door. Marlais called Pat's number again. Damn her, she was probably at her stupid job. Now, when she needed her. Now that everything was obvious.

Constance Berg had been a devoted reader of *The Salon*. So she had read Marlais's review. Had thought the criticism was so incisive that her career was over. Had committed suicide because of it.

No, no. Surely she had gotten bad reviews before.

But not like this, Marlais thought. No, not like this.

· · ·

Marlais was walking but without the dog. Marlais walked past the grocery store with its fruits and vegetables, away from the dirty river toward the library. In the foyer, it took her a moment to decide how to find what it was she wanted, but she quickly opted for the rows of computers to the left of the circulation desk. She looked up reviews and commentary about the work of Constance Berg. She had to use a poorly organized set of CD-ROMS, and even microfiche, but after a while she had a stack of papers. She read the reviews, word by painful word. Most of them were pretty good. A few were glowing. A few struck Marlais as odd, as if the reviewer wasn't reviewing the book that Marlais had recalled reading. Which made Marlais want to read the author's books again. All thirteen.

She had two at home.

The library had six, but that included the two she had.

She purchased the rest. Pat had to special-order them.

She read and reread them.

She started to collect obituaries. Tributes. Although she researched the library several times, there were fewer than Marlais would have thought. After all, this author was a famous writer! A master of her craft. A writer's writer. The best writer of her generation.

Marlais e-mailed *The Salon* and pitched a tribute to Constance Berg.

"Check out volume three, number five" came the reply.

Marlais responded that she intended to do something longer, more substantive, sort of a retrospective but also a critique engaging the reviews of Berg's thirteen books.

No reply came.

Marlais decided that she was going to dedicate her novel to the memory of Constance Berg.

She knew Anna Karenina would not mind being supplanted.

She thought Pat would understand.

The only trouble was, Marlais couldn't write.

Her retractable-point Namiki fountain pen had ink that

would not flow. Her notebook with real wildflowers pressed into its handmade paper cover seemed too delicate for anything she might write. The computer screen was a gray hole, the back side of a cheap mirror, the magic flecked off and chipped.

The manuscript in her rattan box stayed the same for a while; she could not seem to add any pages to its bulk. And then it started to lose sheets. As Marlais reread what was once her wonderful novel in an attempt to find her way back to her own words, she culled. A few sentences at first, then whole pages, then entire scenes, the first chapter, the last.

She measured every word of her own against the thirteen books of Constance Berg and found every word of her own paltry. Or excessive.

There was one night, not an especially dark night but definitely night, when Marlais thought about suicide. She wondered how she would accomplish it. Not by walking off the roof; she knew that. And nothing in the bathtub; that was too inconsiderate of whoever might find her. Ditto the gun in the mouth or temple, not to mention the fact that she didn't have a gun. The river seemed too dirty and hanging seemed too precarious. Pills, Marlais determined, definitely pills.

Anna Karenina whined at the door.

There would be no one to walk the dog. Marlais sighed.

So she decided to live, at least as long as Anna Karenina did.

Though she knew she would always be as unhappy as she was now. Now that she could no longer write. Now that she had just about lost Pat with all her rants and her obsessive readings of Constance Berg's books. Now that she had published some silly review that would rewind in her head every day of her life.

And even if Marlais could see the future—that she would live in a long and settled and even lustful relationship with a woman who was working with Pat at the bookstore; that she would go to graduate school and eventually become a popular professor of American literature; that in her book jacket photograph she would look serious and yet sensuous with a flash of silver ring at her neckline; that her biography of Constance Berg would be a critical and a popular success—she knew it would never be any different.

His Sister

No matter what else anyone knows about Jolene Fields—her red hair that spirals from a heart-shaped head, her lust for eating chocolate and pizza, her lesbianism—once someone learns about her brother, everything else is eclipsed. Her brother has the power to define her, just as he had when they were younger, living in the Okeechobee scrub, their mother working in a resort for retirees and their father long gone. Even now that Jolene is also long gone, gone north like the rumors of her father. Long gone to college and then going on for another degree; long gone until she found herself standing in the hallway of an apartment house holding a letter saying that she had passed the bar and a few days later standing in that same hallway holding a telephone receiver listening to a job offer. Long gone into a life as the director of the Criminal Defense Resource Center, her voice calming criminal defense attorneys all over the Empire State from her little office in Albany for more than ten years.

The job is perfect for Jolene. Her favorite part of law school was the research; her least favorite part was the mock trial, during which her panty hose clung to her thighs and she stuttered in front of the retired judge. She loved "Criminal Procedure" and "Evidence;" she hated "Wills," "Trusts," and "Commercial Paper." She often feels amazed at the privilege of being able to "do" criminal defense work and never walk into a courtroom.

"Jo," some criminal defense attorney in Buffalo or Brooklyn, in Rochester or Syracuse, in Columbia County or Manhattan, will sigh when he or she hears Jolene's voice on the other end of the line. "I'm in trial," the attorney will explain. "I need it quick," the attorney will whine. If Jolene doesn't already know the answer to the question, she can get it before the ten-minute recess is over. Jolene, with her memory for case names and citations and modifications on appeal, with her ability to translate a hunch into a query to be fed to a hungry legal database, with her no-bullshit answers, is well regarded. She's a "state treasure" and a "lawyer's lawyer," at least according to the presenter of her award at the Criminal Defenders Association annual meeting, the year before last.

And everyone clapped. Her colleagues, who she suspected actually thought less of her because she did not fight in those trenches known as courtrooms, all applauded. Over the years, she had saved each of them from the wrath of some former-prosecutor-now-judge at least once. Not only that, she wrote many of their appellate briefs, especially the winning ones.

Sure, a few of the applauding attorneys, all of them men, had been a bit disappointed when they actually saw Jolene walk up to the stage to retrieve her award and smile at the organization president. Yes, a few of the men had imagined that she would be silky somehow, or at least wearing a silky dress in mauve or burgundy, something that matched their vision of her voice. They never pictured her with her feral red hair, or dressed in a pair of black jeans and a black turtleneck and a blazer. Though a few of the women, quite a few of them, found Jo's voice even more comforting and commanding after they saw her. And as unprofessional as it was, a few of them managed to telephone her when they happened to be in Albany, just for a cup of coffee or dinner, and if something else developed, well, that would be fine too.

It was more often than not that something else developed. The women who had seen her receive the Criminal Defenders

Association award and, taking a chance, had called her, gradually gained membership in a very unofficial organization that might have been called the Jolene Occasional Appreciation Club. For almost as many years as Jolene had been at her job, she had been joining visiting women attorneys in their rooms at the Omni Hotel of Albany, where she ordered pizza from room service and ate the chocolates in the minibar and let women loose their fingers in her hair. She was generally judged a considerate lover, if a bit overathletic for a few of the downstate attorneys. She possessed a wide range of attractions, liking all sorts of women. She had no preferences for a certain color of eyes or hair, for a particular shape of breast or hip, for a race or nationality. She did not even prefer attorneys, although she liked to joke she met most women "at the bar," which included the queer bar as well as the profession. But mostly Jolene stayed clear of the queer bar. Not because it was rowdy or because she was getting to be a good deal older than most of the other patrons, although both of these things were true. But because the women who patronized the local bar tended to be, well, local. Women who had no reason to stay at the Omni Hotel; women who might invite her to dinner at their apartments; women whom she could see leaning out their car windows, waving a greeting, while Jolene was walking into her office building, or a grocery store, or even the Omni.

Another of Jolene's jokes, recounted to women who often failed to appreciate the humor, was that what was wrong with women was that they didn't appreciate the limits of intimacy. Laughing and futilely smoothing a ringlet of her almost-maroon hair, Jolene resorted to such quips when she sniffed words like *love, relationship,* and *commitment* perfuming the air. Jolene did not enjoy being crude (although she reassured herself that she was being subtle), but what she had always hated about women, and hated still, was the way in which they equated intimacy with details, almost as if women believed that knowing the brand of peanut butter she used, or the color of her socks, or the date of her birth, or the name of her first lover and how they met could be accreted into a foothold into her soul. And when she was stingy with details, answering even direct questions with a shrug or a joking retort, some women persisted, accusing her of being withdrawn or uncaring or—the most accursed of curses—of being just like a man.

Though even the most confrontational and complaining women, once they learned about Jolene's brother, softened. For these women then thought they knew why Jolene had been guarded with them. It wasn't privacy or boredom or perversity. It wasn't insulting. It was that Jo had something worth hiding.

Her brother.

And not just her brother, her twin brother.

Her twin brother is Jefferson Fields.

Jefferson and Jolene. Jolene and Jefferson. She was called Joey and he was called Sonny. They toddled together and giggled together and played strange games while their mother waited for their father to come home. Or at least they must have. Jolene swears she doesn't remember a minute of it. Doesn't recall their older sister Pamela being killed by a drunk driver or their younger sister Annette being born. Doesn't remember the hot, flat days or the nights close with palmetto bug wings. Doesn't know whether Sonny was the kind of kid who tore the legs from lizards, like some people would later testify, or whether he was an asset to the track team, as the coach would say under oath.

Jolene has been assisting on a case lately about a man convicted in Schenectady for child molestation. She is writing the memorandum of law supporting the defense attorney's motion for a new trial based on the admission of the man's confession, detailing certain acts with his nine-year-old daughter. The man has also "confessed" to murdering his therapist, a psychologist who remains very much alive and busy with her lucrative practice in Schenectady. But after an especially intense session in which the therapist said something like "It would be understandable if you wanted me dead," the man insisted that he had pummeled his therapist with a claw hammer.

Jolene has been researching what is called memory enhancement, the psychological experiments in which the subject (Jo loves it when the person is referred to as a subject) is coached to imagine something and then later remembers the imagining as a memory. As the defense theory goes, the man in Schenectady was seeing a therapist about his guilt feelings for not protecting his daughter and somehow got twisted into his confession about the child molestation, the same way he got twisted into his confession about the "murder" of the therapist. The judge, a former prosecutor, is predictably quite skeptical.

Though Jo is not. It makes perfect sense to her. That memory is invented, induced, enhanced, whatever one wants to call it. Which is why she doesn't trust the only three things she remembers about Sonny.

First, there is the time she and Sonny were swimming and they saw what was an alligator—or a log, who could tell?—and Sonny screamed and she put her arm around his neck and "lifesaved" him to the sandy shore of the swimming hole. Her long red hair splayed itself around her neck like an electrician's assortment of copper wires, drying there, while Sonny's head rested against her throat until he finally stopped whimpering.

Her second memory is more about their mother than Sonny, but Sonny's quick breath was slapping her hair as they both listened to Mrs. Van Doren telling Ma that the reason Joey could run faster and climb higher than Sonny was probably because Joey was supposed to be a boy. But, according to Mrs. Van Doren, while the twins were "floating around in the womb," Sonny had broken off a piece of Joey's "not-even-born-yet chromosome" ("them things are pretty frail then," Mrs. Van Doren spoke knowingly) and so Joey had become a girl by accident. And Joey was just about to laugh when she heard her mother say, "I guess you're right, Madge," to Mrs. Van Doren and Joey didn't want to laugh anymore, but wanted to go slap Mrs. Van Doren right across the face.

In Jolene's third memory of Sonny, they are no longer children. It is the most recent and the most dubious. Though it is true that Sonny came to visit her when she was in college. It was winter, she knows that, though whether Sonny really bought a leather coat at a secondhand shop is harder to determine. Just as she can't figure out whether he really crawled in bed beside her and put that heavy calfskin coat over them both and his fingers in her hair and breathed on her neck for the long, long hours until dawn. Whether he said the things she thinks he said, things about the swimming hole and the alligator and her being his lost twin and how sorry he is that he broke her chromosome because all he ever wanted was a brother and what he got was a house full of silly sisters and how their fucking father left them when the moon was full and the bank account empty and how he can recall every single terrible moment of the ugliness of their childhood and how can she just go on as if none of it ever happened when it did, it all did. And Jolene thinks that Sonny was sobbing then, as if he possessed the most horrible hurt in the universe, as if he had irrevocably lost the struggle for happiness. She kept her bones as rigid as she could because they were her fortress, protecting her heart deep in the tower of her body and keeping him far outside the moat of her skin. That's how she remembers thinking of it. Or thinks she remembers.

Because didn't Kate tell her about this? Not only about that cold night at college with the calfskin coat, but also the broken chromosome and her saving Sonny from the alligator. Yes, wasn't it Kate?

Kate, a criminal defense attorney.

But not one of Jolene's attorneys.

One of Sonny's attorneys.

The one who is going around the country, appearing on television and everything, talking about Sonny.

The one who keeps flying up from Florida to Albany to see Jolene, though Jolene always tells her that she's busy. Kate always stays at the Omni and Jolene never visits her there. Though Kate manages to find Jolene. Once even in the Omni lobby with Belinda from Rochester, as Jolene and Belinda were going to Belinda's room and planning to order a pizza from room service. More often at Jolene's office, where Kate talks to everyone she manages to introduce herself to, which is everyone she sees.

Which is how most people know what they think they
know about Jolene. The way they describe her in a whisper to
each other and the way they each think of her. Jolene Fields,
director of the Criminal Defense Resource Center, whose
twin brother is a convicted sexual serial murderer on death
row.

Jolene's red hair, her excellent memory, her passion for
chocolate, her lesbianism, all become negligible. Irrelevant. For-
gettable and forgotten.

The details might be resurrected as intriguing—titillating,
really—if one ever heard from Kate the details of Jo's brother's
crimes. His alleged victims were all redheads. Found strangled,
their naked bodies smeared with cheap chocolates in the apartments they shared with their female roommates. Not one of
the victims was an attorney, although one was a law student.

But most people do not learn these details. Kate does not
divulge them, not from any deference toward Jolene, but simply because these are not the details that Kate marshals in her
defense of Sonny. The world erupts with infinite details, each
sparking for its moment of attention. And the fact that Jolene
Fields, director of the Criminal Defense Resource Center, has a
brother on death row seems detail enough. Why dig any farther into the rubble?

And for those who do want more particulars, what they seem
to want to know is which came first. Just as people would ask her
mother which twin was born first, the girl or the boy. Now they
want to know whether the brother got convicted and then his sister went to law school or vice versa. People generally prefer the
first explanation; it seems tidier. Just as people assumed that the
boy baby was the first out of their mother's womb.

People like order, mistaking sequence for causation. That's
what Jolene thinks about it. That's what she's always thought
about it, at least as far back as she can recall. And she's been
thinking about it more than she has for a long time, probably
since the last time she decided it was time to become long
gone. Though this time, it's a little more involved. She has a
career to quit.

Her resignation requires an explanation. Belinda from Rochester and the other women are asking for one. They are asking her why she is leaving her job as director of the Criminal Defense Resource Center; why she won't be available at the other end of the telephone line for recess questions; why she won't be writing next year's winning appellate briefs. They are also asking, implicitly but equally urgently, why she won't be available for those occasional and passionate nights at the Omni Hotel.

It is not as if Belinda and the other women themselves has not each thought—has not dreamed, planned, and talked—about doing the same thing Jolene says she is doing. About giving up a job they had once wanted and which has become their only chance at celebrity. About moving somewhere, made important by virtue of being "away." To say good-bye to Jolene instead of vice versa.

And it is not as if Belinda and the other women think Jolene's decision is irrational. The job is stressful. The winters are harsh. She has no real relationship. But these things are no different from what they have ever been. These things have been true for as long as they have known Jolene. The only thing that is different is that Jolene says she is leaving.

But the fact that each of them has considered leaving, or that leaving seems a rational choice, does not blunt the demand of Belinda and the other women for some sort of explanation from Jolene. It may even operate to the contrary. Perhaps the fact that Belinda has herself often thought of leaving her criminal defense practice in Rochester (maybe for Majorca, she has mused) makes Belinda even more desperate for Jolene's explanation. Perhaps the judgment that Jolene is simply being sensible makes the other women even more anxious, because that might mean Jolene hasn't been sensible before, or that they are not being sensible now.

Jolene, hearing the craving that is not adequately masked by Belinda's polite inquiries, listening to the need in the voices of the other women, struggles to provide a suitable story. Jolene is not a cruel woman. And now that she thinks she is leaving Belinda and the other women, believes she will never spread her hair against their thighs, framed by the bright white sheets of the Omni Hotel in Albany, Jolene wants to please them one last time.

Jolene's efforts produce three possible reasons, which she outlines for herself as if she is constructing the arguments on appeal.

First, there is Kate.

As Kate is telling everybody, Kate is a woman in love.

It happens more often than Jolene would have thought, though everyone who has been in the business for more than a year or two has seen it. It seems to happen most often with female attorneys. An argument for not having women attorneys, Jolene knows. Once she would have had her counter-argument, pointing out the assumption of heterosexuality, but then she'd heard about that dyke attorney in Ohio who had fallen for one of her clients. And fallen hard. Gave up her lover and her career to devote all her energies to getting this triple murderer a new trial or clemency or something.

And it had happened to Kate.

Kate is in love with Sonny, who she usually calls Jefferson or even Mr. Fields, and is, of course, absolutely convinced of his innocence. Kate will appear on any television, radio, or on-line program that will have her, declaring her love and Sonny's virtue in the same breath, as if they were two sides of the most obvious equation. Kate says she is going to marry Sonny. There is a delay in getting the Department of Corrections permission, but the real delay seems to be Kate's negotiations with a television newsmagazine that might be willing to broadcast a live segment of the ceremony.

The second reason is New York.

After more years than anyone can recall, the New York legislature has passed a capital punishment statute and district attorneys are beginning to seek the death penalty for defendants. Soon—Jolene can smell it the way she could always smell a hurricane coming across Lake Okeechobee—attorneys will be telephoning her with questions about challenges to prospective jurors who have expressed some hesitancy about capital punishment, questions about aggravating and mitigating circumstances, questions about the standards on a petition for a stay of execution. Jolene doesn't know that law, doesn't know those cases.

And doesn't want to know them.

Third and last is Sonny. Though first and second is also Sonny, Jolene would admit. But third and last is *really* Sonny. Jefferson Fields, inmate on Florida's death row, is running out of appeals. The governor keeps signing death warrants with Sonny's name. And just about everybody who has been on death row longer than Sonny has been executed. Most of the people who think about these things think that Sonny is next.

Sonny is also thinking he is next. Or if not next, soon. And he's been making plans. Plans that include who he would like to witness the execution on his behalf. Witnesses who sit behind a glass partition, looking at the inmate being strapped into Florida's electric chair, known as Old Sparky, and watching the hood being placed over the inmate's head and seeing the switch being pulled. If everything goes well, the inmate stiffens, then slumps, dead. When things don't go so well, the electric current needs to be sent a few times, the body being jerked around for several minutes until death arrives. Or there is some sort of shortage and the inmate's mask catches on fire. The witnesses can't prevent any of this; they can only witness it. Witness it when it is happening and then later to reporters and then every night for the rest of their lives.

Kate, as Sonny's attorney and perhaps his wife by then, will be there. And he has asked his sister, Jolene. She is, after all, a rather obvious choice, the inmate's twin sister, a criminal defense lawyer in New York. Though in his letter asking her to be a witness, Sonny doesn't mention her professional status. He writes about how she saved his life from the alligator, how he's sorry he broke her chromosome, and how he never, ever wanted to hurt her, not even during that night in bed together with a leather coat he got her, in her apartment when she was in college and her skin smelled like chocolate.

Jolene rips up the letter.

Jolene never shares this third reason with Belinda or the other women. And she never mentions her first reason, Kate, although Belinda does remember Kate from the Omni lobby. No, armed with her three possibilities, Jolene always chooses the second. The state of the law in New York. She lets her proffered rationale hang in the air. Let the listeners make the connection to Sonny, as they eventually will do.

Jolene is using her brother and she knows it.

Because Jolene also knows that none of her three reasons is true. Each of her three reasons is simply an argument. And she can refute each of them.

Kate is a nuisance but harmless, without a real effect on Jolene.

New York's implementation of capital punishment will be an intellectually challenging area of the law if she chooses to learn it, but as the director of the Criminal Defense Resource Center, she can easily avoid it by assigning it to someone else in the office.

Sonny can be refused, not even replied to. What is he going to do, turn up at her door this winter wearing a leather jacket?

It could be that simple.

But Jolene wants it even simpler.

As simple as forgetting she was ever his sister.

Jolene wants to walk into a bar—one that sells liquor—and be identified as the woman with the wild red helixes of hair twisting from her heart-shaped face. To become known, gradually and delicately, for a certain style of athletic passion and an endearing emotional reticence. Until her reputation spreads into tales of chocolate and pizza—and not a breath farther.

Atlantis V

*T*hat's the name of the condominium where she lives. She tells him because he has asked whether she lives on the island. They are meeting each other for the first time, though there is an inexplicably sharp familiarity to each of them about the other. They are at a reception for the grand opening of a branch of Sun Bank, busy and bored with their task of making an appearance.

"It's really amazing how much this bank has grown. I remember when it was a tiny operation, and then it got the Disney World account, and now its orange logo is all over the state."

"Do you work for the bank?" she asks. She looks at the earring in his left ear, nostalgic for the time when a little gold hoop could be a symbol of something.

"No, in fact, most of the time I work against them. But now I'm trying to work with them. Well, actually, it's still against them but it should seem like it's with them, though I think they really know it's against them. I guess that sounds confusing."

She angles her head in a gesture he interprets as agreement.

"I'm a lawyer doing CED," he continues. "Community Economic Development. You know, giving the land back to the people, minorities, the poor, the disenfranchised. Your basic sixties agenda." His attempts at humorous self-effacement are sometimes effective, but this is not one of those times. She is looking at him evenly, no shimmer of smile evident on her sharp face. They stand in awkward silence, queued in the line that moves slowly toward the weakly spiked punch.

When they get their plastic glasses, they do not part. They are drawn together by more than the fact that neither one of them can spot anyone else in the room who would be less troublesome to talk with than present company. Their banalities continue as they exchange small bits of information dispersed in their words almost as thinly as the gin in the pinkish liquid they sip. Not quite as lackadaisically as the liquor smooths their discomfort; they are each becoming interested in the conversation—not the conversation they are having but in some subterranean communication that is gathering force. Whenever it threatens to erupt, they are joined by some free-floating third person who rushes toward their magnetic field.

This time it is Stash, a man he has known all his life by sight, but knows less about than the occasional waves of gossip, none of which he can recall at the moment.

"Hey, Clay, que pasa?" Stash's inflection admits no accent marks.

"Not much," says Clay.

"Aren't you going to introduce me?" Stash winks at Clay. "I can always count on you to be with the most gorgeous female in any room. One of life's little ironies."

Clay looks at the woman to see whether she is gorgeous. He's not sure; thinks he's not the one to judge. Certainly, she could be described as imposing. She is a white woman who stands about six feet tall. Her 173-pound frame includes large bones that protrude in unlikely places and ash-blond hair, which she usually ties severely in some sort of braided knot or keeps scarfed. Her eyes are not really blue, but a North Atlantic gray rendered more tropical by the tinted contact lenses she wears. She seems more angular than she is because she holds her long neck as straight as her spine. She is the kind of woman, Clay thinks, that a man will notice when she walks into a room, and will be sure that she does not notice him.

Clay turns toward her to rush through the nuisance of introductions. He realizes then that he knows where she lives, knows she prefers sailing to surfing, knows she has never been to Disney World and has no plans to go, but that he does not know her name.

"Andi Green," she says, extending her hand almost graciously. She looks at Clay as if she has delivered him from some torture and expects to be repaid.

"You're not letting this guy con you, are you?" Stash slurs as if he has consumed gallons of the punch, or else came to this function already fortified. "Don't believe a word he says. Old Mr. Zapato here thinks he's better than the rest of us just because he's a lawyer. Well, he isn't. His old man was a fisherman just like mine, though not as good. You'd better believe that." Shifting his attention to the woman, he asks, "Are you one of the girls with the bank?"

"No. On both counts."

"What?"

"I said no. I'm not a girl and I'm not with the bank."

Clay cannot tell whether or not Stash is embarrassed, although it really does not matter because Clay is embarrassed enough for both of them. It seems absurd to him to refer to Andi as a girl, not only for the usual reasons, but also because there is nothing remotely childlike about her. Then there is the assumption that she is with the bank; an assumption with which Clay feels slightly uncomfortable, even as he realizes it could be true for all he knows.

"Then what are you doing here? Did you come for all the free food? Just look at that spread."

Clay gives up any hope that Stash can be chagrined.

"Someone I work with is on the board of directors."

"Oh. So, where do you work?"

"At the St. Lucie plant."

"The nuclear power plant?" Stash asks.

"Is there another one?" Andi answers.

Clay is attempting not to be appalled. His general political stance includes an opposition to nuclear power, a subject about which he knows very little except that an accident in the reactors less than ten miles from his home could kill him and everyone else instantly. This is enough knowledge, he thinks. But Clay also prides himself on being an economic realist; when times are hard, people take jobs wherever they can get them. He knew lots of fishing captains who signed on to construction jobs for the plant back in '71 when the fishing was poor and the prices were low. Still, it seems to Clay that Andi could probably get a job elsewhere if she really wanted. He would like to know exactly what Andi does at the plant, but he does not want to ask because he had not asked her about her work before and does not want to seem confrontational now. Clay is always a bit squeamish about people's occupations. He likes to pretend, especially to himself, that people's livelihoods are incidentals shaped by the vagaries of circumstance and economy rather than by character. His curiosity is relieved by Stash's conversational inquiry about Andi's precise function for Florida Power.

Actually, she throws away a half smile. "I don't work for Florida Power. I'm with EPRI—Electrical Power Research Institute. I'm here on a consulting contract."

"On what?"

"Health concerns."

"Oh. You're a doctor." Stash sounds a bit disgusted.

"No. I'm a physicist. A nuclear physicist with a specialty in health physics."

"Oh, shit," Stash mouths.

"Is there a problem with the plant?" Clay interjects.

"No. No problems. Routine assessments." Andi takes a sip of the punch from the plastic glass.

"Well, then. You must have some free time. How about a date? Dinner or something?" Stash steps closer to Andi.

"No, thanks. I'm not much for dating."

Men. Clay thinks he hears the word *men* float in the air. Not much for dating men.

"I'm not married," Stash protests. "I'm separated. Legally separated."

"No, thank you. Married or not."

"Oh." Stash retreats finally, but turns around after a few steps and says, "Sorry I interrupted. I guess I see now what you two have in common. Must be lots to talk about."

Andi raises her eyebrows at Clay.

Clay tries to raise his own eyebrows back, but it's not something he does effectively. "He probably figures that since you won't go out with him, you're not interested in men. Could there be a finer specimen?" Clay waits for Andi's laugh, but he doesn't have the nerve to wait too long until he adds, "I'm not only the resident radical, I'm queer to boot."

"The word *queer* is rather petulant, don't you think?" Andi takes another sip from her plastic glass.

"I've never thought it was petulant, no. Obnoxious, maybe, but that's sort of what I like about it."

"What's the point of being obnoxious?"

"For the fun of it?" Clay asks her, laughing.

Andi's laugh in quick reply is like something spilling from the glass she is still holding, cascading down to the muted orange carpet, puddling near her shoe, which she moves ever so slightly to cover the spot. As if it were an accident; as if it never happened.

But something happened because before she leaves, they have agreed to meet for dinner. Not a date, certainly, but a tentative attempt at connection. Accompanied by some vague promises to explore the relationship between community economic development and nuclear power consulting.

Clay is always punctual. He knows exactly where her condominium nests in the wave of buildings that follows the slight curve of the coast. He remembered when it was built, another ugly-looking fortress in the war of beach access. Florida had the best laws in the nation, but they weren't good enough to keep the big developers busy in other states.

And it was an out-of-state construction company. Only the local subcontractors made any money on it, and not as much as they were promised. The bank, Sun Bank, had made a bundle, between the construction loans and the mortgages. Clay had wanted to dynamite the damn thing.

But instead he had represented a small subcontractor whose bid was rejected, settling out of court for a negligible sum.

Thinking then, and most of the times he drove past it, that he was in the wrong profession. He should have been a saboteur, not a public interest lawyer.

He knocks on the door of her fifth-floor unit.

He is not as she remembered him. This man is just her height; the man she remembered was taller. This man's beard has scraggly patches and his pale eyes are slightly bloodshot behind gold aviator glasses. He does not wear the earring she remembered. His shirt seems to have shrunk, or perhaps it never fit. It rides over the waistband of his not altogether comfortable-looking jeans. He is just another overgrown white boy, she thinks, wanting to lock herself into either of the two bathrooms in her condo.

However, she assumes she made some gesture of invitation, because here he is walking through her living room as if pulled by the ocean beyond and below the sliding-glass doors. He stares at the water a moment, as if he is seeing it for the first time, although he cannot remember his life inhabiting the space of even a single second before he had seen the sea. In fact, his mother had brought him to the public beaches when he was a few weeks old. His father was a fisherman, one of the descendants of the Basque who left their mountainous inland homeland and produced progeny adept at trolling Florida's eastern shores.

The view from Andi's living room is spectacular, though no more spectacular than the one he had just left at his own place, perhaps even less so. He puts his fingers in the door notch to slide the glass away, intending to step out onto the terrace.

"Don't go out there," she says, alarmed.

He reels himself back to a world in which defects in construction have legal remedies and asks her whether the balcony is unsafe.

"No," she replies with a coldness that insists that he turn his back to the semitropical Atlantic and the inviting terrace. He retraces his steps back into rooms that now seem absolutely icy to him. The decorating scheme, he thinks—if one can call it that—is, in fact, the color of icebergs. The walls are predictably white. The wall-to-wall carpeting is an impractical white. There is a geometrical-looking couch that is white and adorned with five undersize white throw pillows. There is a single white armchair with a fluted back. There is a clear Lucite coffee table, its iridescent surface unfettered by objects. The dining room table is made of a similar clear material and its two chairs are fashioned from white pipe in a style that Clay recognizes as high tech. He cannot imagine Andi's large frame being restfully supported by those contortions called chairs. Clay's furtive glance into her bedroom, with its large window on the ocean, reveals a bed without a headboard draped in a white chenille bedspread. He can also see a white lacquer dresser without a mirror.

It takes a few lengthy seconds for Clay's usually acute perceptions to register the most startling feature of these rooms: what they lack. There is no television set (which he approves) and no stereo system (which he finds unbelievable). There is nothing on the walls, no knickknacks, no books and no bookshelves. There is not a leaf of green, either artificial or otherwise.

Clay is relieved only slightly from the unsettling starkness of his surroundings when he sights a white ten-speed bicycle in the kitchen. It, at least, seems to speak of something human as it leans propped against the wall while Clay searches for an explanation to satisfy his eeriness. He knows she's been living in this condo for about a year, so he discounts the plausibility of all the accoutrements of her daily life waiting to be unpacked in boxes in her closets. He also rejects any monetary reasons. She is a professional woman with a well-paying job. Besides, Clay has been in enough homes of the marginally poor to know that the lack of money often manifests itself in a greater number of possessions rather than fewer. His clients' homes, as well as the tiny house where he grew up, are stuffed with the secondhand. He knows too well the worn rugs over the holes in the floor, the thin cushions on the teetering chairs, the broken toasters, plastic Parsons tables, cracked bowls filled with stray screws and bits of fishing line. He knows about boxes of pillowcases saved for the company that will never arrive, just as one pillowcase print will never match the pattern of any other. He has stared at the walls scarred by tacks that hold up the overlapping and water-stained pictures: family portraits, family politics and attempts to capture the beautiful and weave it into the fabric of family life.

Now he is staring at the rooms, thinking he is alone in a dream of his own making because he does not see Andi. He listens to the breathing of the ocean, muffled through the heavy glass. His eyes skim over her shadowless form and then return when he realizes there has been a twinge of motion near the dining room table. She looks like a piece of the missing furniture, perhaps a hutch with all the dinnerware removed for cleaning. She is wearing a white cotton oversize shirt that is fashionable this year over white cotton pants of a crop length that is also fashionable this year. Her shoes are white cotton ones from China, like the black ones that had been the fad several years ago. A white turban is carefully wrapped on her head and she is without jewelry.

He would like to leave by the back door, but since this condo does not have one, he considers for a moment opening the door to the terrace and jumping onto the beach. Instead, he dives into the evening.

"I thought we might go to a nice fish place I know of. It's very small and casual, but the catch is always fresh. I know the guys—"

"I don't eat fish."

"Well, how about that Japanese steak house. It's a chain, but—"

"I don't eat meat."

They settle for a new Italian place because it boasts fresh pasta. It is the last thing that night which is so easily settled.

It is still dark as she steps onto the terrace, her hair loose and her only clothing a white shift with desultory embroidery made in Ceylon. Her body can sense the stars shifting to make room for the sun. She sits with her legs crossed, the back of her hands resting on her knees and her hands slightly cupped upward. She begins to relax herself—first her toes, then her heels. She is at her knees when she begins to free herself of her numerous quarrels with the procedures at the St. Lucie Power Plant. It is not until her stomach—her solar plexus, to be more accurate—that she can cast off last evening's episode with Clay Zapato. It annoys her that it takes her this high into her body to shake him off. It is not until she stretches for the top of her spine that she is able to disperse her annoyance.

Once relaxed, her breathing deep and bottomed, she throws a thinly webbed silver net around her spirit for protection. Then, while sitting perfectly still, she leaves the terrace for the surf. She walks out into the water, which rushes around her ankles and then her calves, and though she walks farther and farther, the water never rises any higher. She walks and walks eastward, until she is exhausted. When she feels she will drop, she is rescued from the unremitting blue glare of her world by the circling gulls. Then she is walking toward the smooth coast. She is no longer tired as she trots on the gentle sand, feeling as if she has never been gone.

The brilliance of the no-longer-reddish sun rising from the place the sea and sky meet makes her eyes open. She rises with it, feeling both refreshed and fatigued. She shakes out the white towel over the railing, folds it neatly on the chair, and leaves the terrace for her morning shower.

• • •

There are exactly fifteen dresses in the walk-in closet in Andi's bedroom. There are no skirts and one jacket. There are four blouses with labels that say 100 percent cotton and four slacks with similar labels. There is a pair of crop pants, white. There is one shift, one bathrobe, and one beach cover, also white. On the closet floor, in a neat row, sit four pairs of shoes, including a pair of running shoes and a pair of sandals. In the drawers of a white lacquer dresser there are seven sets of underclothes, two pair of shorts, a pair of running shorts, a leotard, two bathing suits, and one pair of sweat socks.

She puts on the red dress with a white collar that she will wear to work today. It is not until she is in the control room of the power plant, collecting elaborative data from engineers and discreetly picking at the unraveling hem of her dress, that her morning meditation erupts into her consciousness. She notices a red welt in her mind that she can call nothing other than Clay.

So, she calls him. She tries to be guided by her meditations and has found that she ignores them at her peril. They are neither dreams nor reality, but worlds that inhabit her when she stills her attachments to her present life. She cannot always remember them clearly, but she is working on that.

She is not sure that she believes that meditations can lead to past-life regressions. A tarot reader told her that. Andi had been vacationing at a beach resort and on a whim she had stopped at the tarot reader's booth. Well, not exactly a whim, but something more like a suggestion, placed in her mental list of interesting things to do by the woman with whom she had spent the night. A cop, no less. Although she hadn't been in uniform when she approached Andi at the bar.

The tarot reader looked at the cards she had turned faceup, some of which—Andi could swear—looked as if they had televisions on them. The reader had sighed and had advised Andi to stop her struggle to be happy.

"I'll never be happy?" She had tried to look alarmed. She assumed she knew what came next: The reader would advise that she purchase some very special candles—for at least one hundred dollars apiece—and then, perhaps, she might have a chance at happiness. Instead the tarot reader said, "That's not what I'm saying. I'm saying it's the struggling that makes you unhappy."

"That sounds awfully Zen," Andi had replied.

The tarot reader had smiled then. Smiled in a way that made Andi think of kissing her. And more.

But the tarot reader had made oblique comments concerning the necessity of compensating for former behaviors and learning to correct karmic tendencies, while being mindful of the dangers of overcompensation. And then had asked Andi if she meditated.

"Yes, I've just started," Andi replied, though she hadn't meant to be so honest.

"That's good. You need to."

"Do you?" Andi risked a personal question.

"No. I see things without needing to meditate."

"Oh? And what do you see when you look at me?" Andi knew she was being flirtatious.

"I see last night."

Andi blushed but tried to recover. "Well, she recommended you. Are you friends?"

"She's my girlfriend," the tarot reader said. And got up from the table, standing, until Andi left.

It all had a simple explanation, Andi knew. The cop and the tarot reader were in cahoots. It was that simple. But Andi couldn't figure out their scam. There was no plea for expensive candles, no further request of any kind. Perhaps, she flattered herself, she was simply not a good mark. Too smart, too invulnerable.

Andi didn't understand it.

What she does understand is that if she misses a morning meditation, her day is marked by slippages into confusion and irritability.

She and Clay make a date for a bicycle ride. The scheduled Sunday arrives with perfect weather, though Andi is a bit addled because of her brief morning meditation which delivered no feeling of calm. They meet in the parking lot of Andi's condominium and point themselves northward at Andi's instigation. Single file, hugging the dunes that bridge the well-traveled road and the ocean, they pedal gracefully. They are protected from the sun by the tall and tropically soft pines.

Though conversation is impossible between the two riders, Clay's feelings of delight are shrinking as he watches Andi sprint ahead of him, until she is a dot on the straight road ahead. It is not that Clay cannot keep up with the speck that is getting smaller and smaller, it is that he is upset that she sets the pace without bothering to consult him. He had wanted a leisurely ride through the flat countryside. He likes to pretend he is bicycling in southern France or Bimini, even as he is relishing the fact that he lives on this not yet completely developed island off the Atlantic Coast of Florida.

She stops near the power plant. When he arrives, steadfastly refusing to hurry, she is smiling and sweatless. She is spreading out a bamboo beach mat and opening a thermos bag. She produces nuts, bananas, grapes, pieces of black bread with cream cheese and two bottles of imported spring water. It is a lovely surprise, but Clay is baffled by two things: where she got this food, since she obviously did not have the bag strapped to her bicycle, and why she chooses to picnic so close to the tons of warm, iridescently blue water rushing from the power plant into the sea.

Clay notices that Andi is more casual than she has ever been in his presence, so he wants to avoid even the hint of controversy the voicing of his questions might engender. He decides to forgive her for racing ahead; decides that she only wanted to surprise him with the food.

Clay surveys his surroundings carefully, thinking this is what he is expected to do. He sees the twin towers that could be mistaken for silos; the pipes; the land empty of vegetation; the workers' cars; the fences and fences and fences, all with barbed-wire necklaces. He walks along the road to silently read the huge promotion plaque he has driven past thousands of times without stopping. It is the propaganda he expects, giving the history of the area and the plant as it touts the safety of nuclear power. He wonders what some future generation might think of these words; these lies that the community accepts nuclear power; these platitudes that the plant must be a good neighbor because "we live here too."

Walking back to Andi, he reads aloud another sign: "Disturbing Sea Turtles in Any Way Is a Federal and State Offense. PENALTY $20,000 Fine and/or 1 Year in Jail."

"What a joke." Andi's voice is raspy.

Clay assumes Andi is going to spoil the delicate balance of his emotions by a comment that sea turtles are oversized, ridiculous throwbacks to a prehistoric age. This is true, Clay thinks, but irrelevant. Clay can remember a time when the sea turtles crawled up the beach in droves on summer nights to lay their eggs near the dunes. He did not have to pester his parents to take him to watch the loggerheads and green turtles. It seems to him now that they must have gone to the dark beach every night. He remembers how the glint of the turtles' tears would be reflected in his father's flashlight, as the turtles strained to lay their silvery eggs. His mother told him that the turtles were crying because they would never see their babies again, for after the females became mothers, they crawled back into the sea. These days, the tracks are sparse. Clay looks out his window and onto the beach in the morning to check for the tracks made by the small feet. The tracks are not beautiful, but look as if a single heavy-treaded tire rolled itself out of the surf and then back. Still, if Clay does not see evidence of turtles, his summer day is tainted.

"Florida Power and Light," Andi continues, "should be going to jail or fined or both, if that sign is for real. This pretty water is full of radwaste. It's also too hot to be dumped back into the ocean. Sometimes I have visions of mutated, radioactive turtles rising from the sea to take over the world like a science fiction movie."

"Are you studying the sea turtles?" Clay is being cautious, as if he has a recalcitrant witness on the stand in an important case.

"No. My research is limited to the unusual."

"What do you mean?"

"I mean that certain things are taken for granted, are

acceptable. I just measure stuff. Rads found in the all-leather soles of secretaries' shoes, for example."

"Well, what if you find it's unsafe. Can't you do something?"

"What's safe? Besides, I'm no Kathy Silkworm."

"That's Karen Silkwood," Clay says, taking the bait a split second before he sees the silver hook.

"How do you know so much?" Andi laces a smile to her lips, her teeth almost glowing. She senses that Clay is one of those people who can be cornered into an apology for any display of knowledge.

"I don't," he says, more conciliatorily than he intended. "I've just seen the movie. And read the book."

"And so you're another liberal against nuclear power?" She smiles, but Clay is now wary of flashes of white or silver.

"Well, I haven't heard anything from you that makes me think it's so great—or that you think it's great."

They eat the rest of their grapes in silence.

When they mount their bikes for the return trip, she speaks as if the conversation, which is still slightly stinging Clay, had not occurred.

"Let me ask you something," she says. "How much did you pay for that bike?"

"I don't remember," he lies. She has already told him that he paid too much for the Ocean Pacific shorts he is wearing; she knows a place where they are much cheaper. She has already inquired about the price of his Top-Siders, forcing him into a confession that they are not Sperry Top-Siders, but some imitative brand.

She motions for him to lead the way and he gladly complies. Yet not even a quarter of a mile past the bridge over the discharge canal connecting the power plant to the sea, she passes him. She disregards the rushing car that swerves into the other lane to avoid her. She pedals furiously, as if she is trying to escape something, he thinks, or else pursuing something that barely eludes her.

Clay's pace is lingering by comparison. He feels entitled to the slowness that self-pity often breeds. He cannot believe he lets people treat him this way. He is a lawyer, a successful lawyer with principles. He thinks that because he is not ugly or fat or diseased or poor, he cannot excuse her lack of consideration. Correcting himself, he decides that even if he were any of those things, he would deserve better treatment. People are people, he thinks. There are certain boundaries of civilized courtesy that must be honored, though he finds it difficult to articulate to himself exactly which rule she has breached.

Clay pumps the bicycle, but he is at his office, trying to draft a complaint against Andi. Not one for court, but one he could express to someone, maybe his mother. Something more substantive than She bicycled faster than me, Mom.

Andi is waiting for him at the entrance to her condominium complex. This time, it is she who reads the sign.

" 'Atlantis Five,' " she says. "Five miles from the power plant. I like to bike briskly."

"Yeah." Clay wonders whether her last statement is offered as an obtuse apology.

"What do you think the five stands for?"

"Maybe it's the fifth building built by the company. Or the fifth building in the Atlantis series of developments."

"No. It's the first venture for this developer. Or at least that's what the condo brochure says."

"Well, maybe there are five partners. Or maybe the president is superstitious and thinks five is a lucky number."

"Five?" She angles her head in a way that suggests their first meeting.

"Yeah. The five senses. The five fingers and toes. The five-day workweek."

"The Pentagon."

They are both laughing.

"Well," he says more seriously, "the ancients considered five very magical: the five races, the five continents, the five seas."

"I thought there were seven seas," she says.

"More than that, actually. A lot of the ancient knowledge isn't considered accurate anymore. Who knows, perhaps the world has changed since then. But five is still kind of mysterious. Five is the future. The fifth dimension. The fifth world."

"What?"

"The fifth world. The Hopi Indians believe we are nearing the end of the fourth world. Though, of course, it remains to be seen whether we make it to number five."

"I thought the Indians believed the world sat on the back of a turtle."

"There are many different tribes of Native Americans," he says, "and each has its own stories. But what's interesting is the similarities between those stories. And not just those stories, but the similarities with the Egyptian and Incan and Etruscan and Hindu."

"How do you know so much?"

He is surprised that Andi's challenge is so soft.

"I saw the movie."

Equaling him, she asks, "Didn't you read the book?"

It is not that Sunday, or the next, or even the next, but some Sunday after that when they maneuver each other into Andi's bedroom between the patternless sheets. It is after a dinner prepared by Andi, consisting mainly, it seems to Clay, of broccoli served in clear glass bowls and claret served in large, delicately etched wineglasses. In addition to the saga of her purchase of the wineglasses, Andi had entertained Clay with anecdotes of her family, the places she has been, and her present job.

They had also argued. About sex.

Clay had pressed her. Pressed her hard. Pressed her because he wanted her to say she was a lesbian. Pressed her hard because he wanted her to be a lesbian.

Instead, she made lofty comments about identity and gender. Postmodern shit, Clay thought.

But he was also mindful of what Stash had said that

evening he had met Andi. Not Stash's clumsy request for a date. Not the implication that Andi was a lesbian, for Clay had already thought that himself. But what Stash said later.

"TV," Stash had said.

And at first Clay had thought Stash was talking about television. And then Clay thought to correct Stash, to say transsexual or transgendered, but Clay didn't know which one was more acceptable these days.

"Natural-born girls aren't that tall," Stash had said.

"A lot of women basketball players would prove you wrong." Clay had tried to keep his voice light.

"Next time you see her, look at her hands and feet. That's what gives them away. I learned that from a program on TV." This time, Stash did mean television.

Clay had shook his head, but found himself at the Italian restaurant, the first time they went out, looking at Andi's hands, snatching glances at her feet. Of course, he realized he didn't have the skills to gauge. He worked with women, but he never looked at their hands or feet and never compared them with men. He knew his own mother's hands, of course, as well as her shoe size, but Basque women were large women. And the men Clay knew, the hands that had touched him and held him and grasped him, were all different sizes. He liked hands as much as the next guy, he thought, though he did not have a particular attraction for them. As long as they weren't too soft.

Too soft was definitely a turnoff. He'd been to parties and bars, mostly when he traveled to Miami or Manhattan or San Francisco or even London, where the men seemed younger and younger and their bodies harder and harder, each man more sculpted than the next. But what he remembered, besides his own humiliation at his ungymed muscles, was his encounter with a very tan and very blond guy with a stone body—hugging him around the waist from the back was like clutching on to one of those rocks the Coast Guard piled on the St. Lucie beach to prevent further erosion—and how the guy's hands had been like those of a baby. Not a callus or a rough spot. The softness had made Clay queasy.

Whenever he left the island, he realized he belonged here. Despite the lack of potential lovers. A lack so pronounced that it allowed him to follow Andi into her bedroom.

Andi is silent. She closes the window because sometimes the ocean sounds like a running toilet to her. She cannot afford to be distracted now. Suddenly she misses the mountains and her childhood. She closes her eyes against the feeling.

When they begin kissing, Clay can feel Andi's passion as well as his own, but knows that the passions will never join. He pictures two parallel lines stretching out to infinity, never finding the place where the universe supposedly curves. Instead, each will measure itself against the other.

Clay abhors competition because he hates to lose. Almost more, he hates to win. In both stances, he lacks grace. As a winner, he pretends his winning is effortless and casual. As a loser, he pretends the result was preordained. After ten years as a lawyer, his stomach still clutches at conflict. He survives an adversarial profession by his insistence that problems are best solved through cooperative socialism. His opponents are often confused. They negotiate with him because they assume he must be more devious than he appears.

Clay's avoidance of competition has become so ingrained that his body gives him no choice with Andi. He cannot make love even if he wants to. And he desperately wants to. At least he thinks he wants to. His desire floats over him like a spirit viewing a corpse. He feels trapped by a piece of flesh.

The question, of course, is what to do with the rest of his body. Should he leave or stay? Andi does not give him any encouragement either way.

In the dawn, she does not roll toward him with coaxing kisses, but scrapes open the window.

"That's so unfair," she says.

He feigns sleep, his paranoia bubbling. He peeks at her pulling on her running shorts. Then she is gone.

And he is going. He mechanically looks out the window to check for turtle tracks and sees two boats surfacing, their nets full of small fish flipping their sliver bodies wildly. So, that's what Andi had meant. He knew she hated the nets. He had told her, rather pointedly, he thought, that people do lots of ugly things to make money.

Turning back to smooth the covers, Clays's foot catches on something under the bed too solid to be underwear. Well, he thinks, it is comforting to know that Andi is not as tidy as she appears. In one swift movement, he is on his knees looking under the bed.

There's a silver box, about a foot square, he would guess, with a hinged lid. He pulls the box from under the bed, pausing a moment to decide whether or not he should look in it. The myth of Pandora scuttles across his consciousness, but it is his conscience that provides the drag on any momentum. It's an invasion of Andi's privacy, to be sure. But somehow he feels that last night's vulnerability gives him a small entitlement. Maybe he wants things to be even. Maybe the box will have embarrassing photographs of Andi as a child, gap-toothed and slovenly and ridiculous in a pinafore and lacy ankle socks. Or maybe documents, divorce papers or diplomas. Or anniversary cards. Or love letters tied with a lavender grosgrain ribbon.

Clay lifts the lid.

A small gasp escapes from his kneeling body.

The box is empty.

The terrace is shedding its darkness and its dampness and giving way to the morning. She is relaxing. Her breathing is growing deeper and her net is being cast. She is doing the breaststroke past waves that ripple gently. She is swimming until she is tired, her limbs heavy.

She is covered in sweat. The rising sun is unmitigated by even a trace of cloud. It is difficult to open her eyes to such a cruelly red horizon, but she must get ready for work. This terrace needs a ceiling fan, she thinks, as she goes inside, carrying the white towel that needs washing.

Of the fifteen dresses in Andi's closet, today is her day to choose the ruby silk with the dropped waist and the slight accordion flare at the hem. She does not simply rotate the wearing of her work dresses, but neither does she submit such an important decision to the vagaries of her postmeditation morning moods. She achieves the desired effect of near haphazardness with the aid of a computer program that amends the random only to the extent of requiring duplicates to be separated by a unit of at least three. Buying a few dresses at the turning of the seasons, she debates which ones to discard in favor of the replacements. Her method of allowing herself no more than fifteen dresses has served her well, though it accounts in part for her preference for assignments to places with predictable weather.

Standing at the narrowest end of the modern, irregularly shaped conference table, Andi feels a little too tart in the presence of the calculated understatement of the men's suits. Perhaps she should resort to purchasing a few suits, she thinks. Perhaps something in a dark navy accented by the palest azure blouse would be sufficient to stun them into listening to her as she gives the oral presentation of her report based on more than two years of research.

Her audience fidgets as she speaks. These slightly tanned men lack discipline, she thinks, as she summons her own to drive her through her words. She has always viewed discipline as the key to life. Without it, she knew she would have wound up as some nondegreed consumer stuffing her house with objects that had no rational purpose save making other people rich. Without it, she knew she would be offering those objects in the futile hopes of ensuring someone else would value her. If it was not for her discipline, she knew she would have fallen in love with someone like that redheaded lawyer from upstate

New York with the brother soon to be executed here in Florida. Or even with a man like the excessively easygoing Clay.

It is self-discipline that makes her career impeccable, her present report a shining example of objectivity and her findings unassailable. Some of her findings should startle them, so restraint is important. She is telling them that she found radiation in doses exceeding the allowable 170 millirems in all the plant workers, including office workers separated from the reactors by containment walls, including some of the executives in the conference room. Not an expression of shock ripples the room. Yet she had not been surprised, so perhaps it is unreasonable to expect her sophisticated audience to register alarm. The impatient postures in the chairs convey their suggestion to Andi that she bring her remarks to a close.

In a pink cotton shirt and matching pale pink slacks, Andi is looking at the books on Clay's shelves. She thinks it is strange that this is the first time she has been to his place, since they have become so close in the past few months, once they both seemed to understand the bounded possibilities of their relationship.

She is amused both by the excessive number of his books and some of the titles.

"*Stonehenge,*" she reads aloud. "*The Maya. The Roots of Civilization. The Fourth Way. Worlds in Collision. The Etruscans. Plato's Dialogues.*

"*La Atlántida Americana,*" she mispronounces. "*Realidad de la Atlántida . . . El Pasado Prehistórico del Gran Peru.* What a mouthful. Hey, I didn't know you knew Spanish."

"With a name like Zapato?"

She juts her head toward him, as if to laugh, but remains silent. She is looking at a reproduction of a map dated 1500. Florida is prominent and labeled, looking like a hugely flaccid piece of flesh hanging off Greenland and attached to China. The only other labeled places include Cuba, Antarctica, Iceland, India, Labrador, Cipango and Atlantis.

"Interesting" is all she says, shifting her view to one of the many windows overlooking the ocean. His floor plan is less like a box than hers, so he has more windows and more views. She fingers a prism that hangs from an otherwise empty curtain rod. Her movements cause the cut glass to cast tiny rainbows around the room.

"And this one?" Andi has picked up a book with a rather lurid title.

"It's a novel. By a friend of mine." Clay is slightly embarrassed. "He's a writer," Clay adds needlessly.

"Is it any good?"

"Well, it got a lot of critical attention, as they say. It was up for this prestigious award. Funded by two lovers who died of AIDS. They were writers also. Novelists, mostly. Though they also wrote this. . . ." Clay takes the novel from Andi's hand and then replaces it with another book.

"*Atlantis*," Andi reads, "*The Autobiography of a Search.*"

"Yeah. They went out in 1968 fortified by lots of marijuana, looking for Atlantis. Found it in Bimini."

"You seem to think they're silly."

"Yeah, I guess."

"Then why do you have the book?"

"My friend, the novelist, gave it to me. Thought I'd like it. Had gotten it when he learned his novel was being considered for the award they funded. He was like that, a researcher. Was probably already planning his acceptance speech."

"Did he win?"

"No. But it didn't matter. He died anyway."

Clay turns toward the ocean, away from Andi.

Andi wants to really talk with Clay. She has a speech prepared. It's not about death, really, but somehow it's related. It begins, "There are some things I just don't understand." She wants to tell him that she is really very spiritual; that she is not merely the careerist she knows he thinks she is. She could take his hands and tell him he is right, she is wasting her life, though he has never said that. But she would also hold his fingers tight and tell him that he is wasting his life too. She does not know what any of her statements would mean, so she does not say them.

Instead she asks him whether he meditates.

"No," he admits. And the truth is that he has tried. Has sat on the beach, has crossed his legs, has closed his eyes, has tried to empty his mind. But it never works.

"You do, I assume."

"Yes, I find it relaxing." Though it isn't always relaxing. That's what she wants to tell him. To tell him sometimes it is terrifying. To tell him it sometimes seems as if she has an alternative life. An alternative life with a brother/lover, a man named Azore, whom she tries to save while their island paradise is being destroyed by nuclear power.

To tell him this: You remind me of this brother, this Azore of my dreams. To ask him this: Isn't there something in all your books that can help me figure out whether I'm just crazy?

She moves to a different set of Clay's bookshelves.

"*Waves and Beaches. Wind Waves: Their Generation and Propagation on the Ocean Surface. Oceanography and Seamanship. Submarine Geology. The Dynamics of the Upper Ocean.* You certainly do like the ocean."

"That's what I majored in at college. I've got a BS in oceanography."

"And you went to law school?" Andi's voice is raspy, rough. "I always had you figured for the sociology type."

This is why, finally, he knows they can never really be friends. It is not because he thinks that she lacks respect for his social conscience. It is not because she can explain to him that she refuses to eat fish, eggs, or milk because plutonium from nuclear waste concentrates in such foods and yet she can cash her paychecks. The real reason he cannot feel close to her is that they have known each other all these months and she did not know until tonight that he is fluent in Spanish, though his ancestry is Basque, which she still does not know. She does not know he gets claustrophobic ten miles inland. She does not know that he does not have a sister; she does not know she produces inexplicable waves of incestuous guilt in him.

Yet what he sees as a self-centeredness in her that does not admit confidences or authentic closeness has not prevented a genuine fondness from growing between them. He knows that her appointment at the St. Lucie Power Plant is coming to an end, and he knows that he will not ask her to stay. She knows that she will be spared attempts to infest her departure with blame.

Their truce glitters in the twilight. They sit on his terrace, different from hers not only because it is twice the size, but because it has furniture, lush plants, and a wicker ceiling fan slowly turning.

"This time of day always seems magical to me," he says, no longer worried that he will be thought silly.

"Twilight? Well, I've always thought dawn to be the top contender in that department," she replies, not turning to see a surprise in his eyebrows that would have been a reward on one of the men in the conference room last week.

There are moments that lengthen like centuries pulling the tide out to sea.

"I can't believe you have all those crazy books."

"I told you I read a lot."

"And see a lot of movies?"

"Not so many movies, actually."

The waves are shadows that lap with their irregular heartbeats.

"Do you really believe in all that stuff in those books about mysteries of the ancient world and stuff?"

"No, not all of it. Not all the facts. Not rich guys in a boat finding Atlantis in Bimini. But I enjoy the myths. Plato started it, actually. Told a tale of a perfect island, a utopia, really, on which people started to become impressed with their own possessions. Became captive to them, almost. Thought they could rule the world. And then the whole business was destroyed by a tidal wave or earthquake. Kind of interesting, when you think about it."

"I guess." Andi's voice is flat.

"And I've always been fascinated with the sea. When I was

a kid, I had this fantasy of swimming clear to the Azores."

"What?"

"Oh, nothing. It's just that I've always felt there was something out there." He gestures in the descending darkness toward the swirling Atlantic. "Something we've lost. Something we need. Don't you think so?"

Andi doesn't know the answer, so she says nothing, and after a while, Clay stops expecting her to.

Women's Music

I pose myself in the darkness of the pre-performance stage and see her face floating in the audience. Tonight, the gig is one of several in San Francisco. I remind myself that as soon as the pink spotlight refracts from the sterling-silver frets of my electric guitar and my voice refracts through the echoplex stacked on the amps, I will forget her; forget that she ever lived; forget that she ever died.

Sometimes I figure that she is merely my personal butterfly, an embodiment of the stage fright that every performer must conquer again and again. Other times, I suppose that it is only natural that I think of Sammy whenever and wherever I take the stage.

Not that Sammy was the one who taught me to sing. No one did that. If that had been necessary, I still would not be able to carry a tune. I was not a child born into a life that could include something like voice lessons. I was a girl who sang every Sunday morning (and Sunday night and Wednesday night) during the Salvation Army services. My mother often appeared in the congregation to cry, especially if my repertoire included "In the Garden" and she had consumed her usual beers and shots. Other women, and a few men, also cried as I sang sometimes. I stretched my soprano down into a raspy bass as I varied my register to fill the church, a small city cellar beneath a pawnshop. I watched the tears slide down the parishioners' faces, like the notes that slipped across the sheet music. I could decipher neither the tears nor the notes, but I was much more intrigued by the notes. I inched closer to Sergeant Haskins, the piano player, because she could translate those circles and lines and stylized flags into messages about where to press her fingers on the keys, where to press her foot on the pedals. There were times, however, that I found the mystery of her breasts bouncing under the worn fabric of her navy blue uniform equally enticing.

Often after Sergeant Haskins was finished pressing ivory keys and metal pedals, she would press my head against her lush breasts. "You sing like the silvery gates of heaven," she would sigh. My voice box would feel like it had melted. Silver, silver, my own voice would whisper in my head. Although I had heard that the heavenly metal was gold, against her breasts I believed silver was the only possible salvation.

Still, I could not convince Sergeant Haskins to reveal the possibility of ivory heavenly gates and teach me to play the piano. She would laugh: "Your voice is a beautiful instrument of God; you should not suffer an instrument made by man." She did not press my head against her breasts when she said this. And she was not pressing my head to her breasts when she told another Salvation Army sergeant that she'd be goddamned if she'd teach that little white nigger to play the piano or else I'd be playing in a cathouse before I was seventeen. I heard her anyway. I leaned against the pawnshop gates a long time that night, just thinking about what she'd said.

If Sergeant Haskins would not teach me voiceless music, there were other women who would. The trick was to find someone who would do it for free. Just as there was no money for voice lessons, there was no money for piano lessons, or for a piano. My mother did not need to explain this to me, or to justify it with an appeal to God. She only needed to hum Patti Page ("Allegheny Moon"), Dinah Washington ("What a Difference a Day Makes"), and Connie Francis ("Who's Sorry

Now?"). She punctuated her impersonations with swigs from her beer bottle.

I finally settled on Gloria, an older girl from the more prestigious edge of the neighborhood. She was from Argentina and her father was the band director at the parochial school for boys. Gloria played the acoustic guitar off the third-floor porch of a tenement, but we worked at imagining her as a lady with a lace mantilla strumming on an elegant European balcony. Gloria worshiped Joan Baez, who—as Gloria explained to me almost every time she mentioned the rapidly becoming famous singer/guitarist—was half Mexican. When she was not talking about Joan, Gloria showed me how to play chords, how to read sheet music, and how to flat-pick a recognizable melody. When Gloria's parents gave her a heavy steel-string acoustic guitar made in Spain ("a lot like Joan's") and a box of tortoiseshell plectrums, Gloria gave me her old nylon-string guitar. She made me cut my nails before she let me try her new steel string, but she still let me try it. She was patient as a Spanish saint as she positioned my fingers with precision, day after day.

Night after night, I slept at her house and she positioned her same nail-bitten hands around my fingers, although with less confidence. The wonderful thing about being a girl in America is the patina of innocence. After delicious rice and bean dinners, we slept together with her parents' blessing and my mother's gratitude. Her parents were happy that Gloria had any friend at all, for Gloria was shy and cross-eyed with perpetually greasy bangs and was interested only in her guitar. My mother was glad that I was not home to interfere with her stupor and not out on the streets inducing my own. So, Gloria and I, sinister schoolgirls, snuggled until sleep overcame us. She kissed me and I let her and I kissed her back. She slid her tongue in my mouth and I let her and I slid mine behind her teeth. Her fingers explored the wet accordion I hid in my underpants and I let her and I explored her. She pressed her tongue past my wet folds and hummed something deep that sounded like "Joanie" and I let her. I did not echo these acts. I was afraid it might ruin my voice.

I never sang for Gloria. I worried that she might cut off my access to an instrument, like Sergeant Haskins did. Or that she might imagine us as a duo: Joan Baez as two people, Gloria with her accomplished guitar, me with my heartbreaking vocal chords. But I knew even then that I did not want to be half of Joan Baez, or even all of her. Years later, one reviewer would christen me with another Joan, calling me the "lesbian Joan Jett," though that was before Jett herself became the lesbian Joan Jett. Another women's publication would canonize me by calling me a "black Janis Joplin," and a rival periodical would enshrine me as a "white Tina Turner." Forget my complexion or even my sexual preference; I am unlike Jett or Joplin or Turner. I never sing about men; I never sing about heartbreak.

Before I ever learned to appreciate Janis Joplin's husky voice overpowering her all-male backup band, Big Brother and the Holding Company; before I ever heard Joan Jett singing, "I hate myself for loving you," while her all-male band, the Blackhearts, jammed behind her; before I ever applauded Tina Turner neé Annie Mae Bullock shafting the abusive Ike, I wanted woman's music that was strong and solid and singular. When I only knew Gloria and the glories of her steel-string guitar, only knew Sergeant Haskins and her ivory gates to heaven, only knew that my voice was silvery enough to make alcoholics weep, I knew I had to make women's music.

When my mother went to the tavern to practice her vocation, I stayed in the two-room apartment and practiced mine. I plugged in her portable record player, strummed my secondhand guitar, and sang along with Brook Benton about the evils of the boll weevil. I sang "Edelweiss" from *The Sound of Music*. I sang "Maria" from *West Side Story*, sometimes substituting Gloria for Maria, as if it would produce more passionate timbres. I listened intently to Herb Alpert's Tijuana Brass, attempting to distinguish the instrument lines and compose appropriate lyrics, but I often got sidetracked by the album cover of the white woman wrapped in a seductive layer of whipped cream.

At every Salvation Army service with a music program, I continued to sing a solo, whether or not my mother was there. The Army was trying to enlist me with litanies of how I could sing the faithful to gates that were now described as pearly. On the more earthly side, the Army guaranteed me an audience for my voice three times a week and lots of time to practice. Perhaps if they would have had more brightly colored uniforms and promised me piano lessons, I would have joined.

Instead, I kept devouring any type of music I could find, looking for women's music. Under the influence of Joan Baez and Gloria, I was practicing the sustained pitch necessary for singing "Amazing Grace" and the bar chords for strumming "We Shall Overcome," when I met Sammy. Sammy sang at one of the taverns my mother frequented. "You have to hear my daughter sing," my mother told me she had told Sammy. "You have to hear this woman sing," my mother told me. My mother seemed to talk to Sammy—and certainly talked about Sammy—as if Sammy were an adult. In fact, Sammy said she was only three years older than me; I figured that lipstick and a sequined dress can make all the difference.

I resisted meeting Sammy, afraid she would hate my voice or my guitar or the kid that I was. It was my mother who brought Sammy to the Salvation Army service one Wednesday night. Sergeant Haskins banged devotedly on the piano I now recognized as out of tune. I spotted Sammy in the congregation as I stood to sing my solo of the Protestantly difficult "A Mighty Fortress Is Our God." It is not much of a tearjerker as hymns go, but several faces were wet nonetheless. Sammy's face was dry. And pale. Very pale.

Sammy was not wearing a sequined dress, but a black sheath that was a little too tight and—surprisingly—a little too long. She reminded me of Morticia of *The Addams Family* TV show, except that her hair was white as my bleached underwear. It was cut bluntly, so that on each side of her face it curved like crooked half smiles into her mouth. When her bare lips parted at my mother's introduction, I could see that Sammy had what cross-eyed Gloria and I called vampire teeth: jutting bicuspids in need of braces.

I thought Sammy was absolutely beautiful.

One look at this woman—and she was a woman even without lipstick or sequins—and I was ready to give up Gloria, eager to abandon Sergeant Haskins. I have always been capable of unfathomable shallowness.

Sammy lived in a room over a tavern. Sammy wanted to put together a rock band, get a recording contract. Sammy had an agent, an eye for costumes, an urge to tour. Sammy slept in a man's size-17 white button-down shirt. She liked to bite hard at that softest spot in my shoulder when we made love. Sammy had a habit. Sammy's voice was decomposing as quickly as day-old shit in the sun.

We became partners. We soon had a backup band with drums and amps and electric guitars. We sang. We danced. We cooled out with the band. The boys talked about riffs and bass lines and stacks. I listened. The boys and Sammy shared drugs during rehearsals. I declined. I wanted not blur, but distinctions; not distortion, but clarity.

And I wanted Sammy, more and more. I wore ripped clothes, not because they fit our band's image, but because I wanted to display my beautiful love bites. I felt weak the mornings after we made love, but I struggled to recover and to bring her coffee. I was jealous of the attention she paid anyone else, even a stray kitten, even the newest guy in the band, the one who would be with us a week or two at most. We never could keep a drummer.

The more I wanted Sammy, though, the more she seemed to want only the blood in the needle. I watched her watch the red rise and fall in the hypodermic. It did have a certain seductive glare, like a thermometer under a tropical sun. But it made me nervous and she knew it. "You just ain't ready," she said. I tried not to be embarrassed. I concentrated on Sammy's mouth, on our music.

Our band, which went through names faster than drummers, got gigs in more and more places; places we could call clubs instead of taverns. Our audience appreciated us by getting drunk on the dance floor and shooting up in the bathrooms. We got paid.

With the money we made, I paid my mother's back rent, bought a totally electric Fender, and splurged on rice and bean take-out dinners. Sammy bought more and more heroin, fresh white roses every day, and stockings with sequins sewn up the sides. I told Sammy the roses smelled as dead as her singing. Sammy told me I played guitar like a Salvation Army reject. We argued more often than not.

On stage, we blew kisses to each other. The specter of what our audience thought might be kinky sex aroused their applause. Sammy wore a white-sequined dress that hugged her pale figure. I refused to wear sequins, but had a satin shirt with satin pants, both in too-tight black. We did not call ourselves Salt and Pepper, but the name came up often. We sang. I always sang louder. We danced. Sammy always danced harder.

During the mandatory keep-the-backup-band-happy, intolerably long instrumentals with the sweaty drum solo, Sammy would shimmer and shake but never strut. I took to picking up my electric Fender and crouching low into my silent chords. I was tolerated as long as I did not plug into an amp.

We changed the band's name to White Roses, at Sammy's insistence. We landed a gig at Trudy Heller's in Manhattan, a well-known hangout of record producers, according to Sammy. We were on the verge of success; we were on the verge of disbanding.

Then Sammy died.

It was Reef, our newest drummer, and the man I suspected of being Sammy's lover, who told me. He was an androgynous sort with long hair and girlish hips. He did not cry, although he sniffed a little. He told me Sammy had overdosed in the apartment of one of their friends that I did not know. I imagined her body, pale and streaked with blood. I tried to think of a question, a detail that would make it more real than a song lyric badly sung.

I wound up writing lots of lyrics about Sammy, most of them bad if not badly sung. Especially bad was "White Roses," which I never sang, except in the shower. One song did make it to the stage: "Every Woman Needs a Dead Lover." It's one of my hits, if any title can be called a hit in the world of women's music.

The pink spotlight hits the sterling-silver frets. I stand in a pool of silence, surrounded by applause. I strum and adjust the tone and volume controls of my expensive electric guitar. At the first chords, the audience stirs with recognition. My voice is distinctively sharp:

> *Every woman needs a dead lover*
> *To be a coldly perfect cover*
> *You can pick up a girl in a bar*
> *Drive her home in your car*
> *Tell her she's a cutie*
> *Lie that she's a beauty*
> *And say: Sorry, I can't love you*
> *It's something I just can't do*
> *The one I love is dead, dead, dead*
> *But let me stroke your pretty head*
> *Safe and warm between my thighs*
> *Let me come and close my eyes*
> *You make me feel like I could die*

I end with a short riff, crouching close to the edge of the audience. The women roar. Sometimes the mere sight of a woman playing an electric guitar is enough to make women yell with appreciation. It's like driving on a lonely road in South Carolina and seeing a woman working heavy equipment.

The song may be shallow and self-serving, as one feminist reviewer judged it, but every audience loves it, or at least they seem to. They also seem to love my equally shallow and self-serving attempt at conversation with hundreds of women.

"It's great to be back in San Francisco."

The women applaud themselves. I do not mention the fog

that eddies around the streets, as if the whole city is nothing other than a set for a spooky movie. I do not mention the sun that never seems to shine, the earth that shudders with unexpected orgasms, the ocean that pounds on the shores, relentless and cold as death.

"Queer capital of the world."

The women applaud themselves again. I cannot see past the glare of the stage lights, but I can visualize the usual crowd: diesel dykes who like the hard drive of my guitar, lipstick lesbians who like the healing bruise of my lyrics. There are women with their lovers, women looking for lovers, and women trying to forget lovers. And all of the women in the audience, in at least a little secret part of themselves, wish they could be me. The women with shy voices and little ambition; the women who watched their brothers play guitar as they took up the clarinet; the women who croon from the depths of their diaphragms and play air guitar as they clean their apartments. The women of my audience.

Before I leave the stage, I want to satisfy each of these women as if I had invited her home for the night instead of making her purchase a ticket to a concert hall. Mostly, I want to make love with my electric Fender, a lighter version of the one I had in the days of White Roses. It is my guitar who is my lover; the lover who will never die. If I smash her, I can replace her. She cannot take up with a male musician unless I sell her.

My last song is always political, still always more rock-vibrant than balladlike. This year I am singing an African freedom song. I am dark enough to ensure a good review.

I sing the song as slowly as possible. I never want to leave my spotlight of safety. The set always ends. I bow and wave and set my guitar down. I leave it there, and walk alone off the stage.

Backstage there will be hand-lettered invitations and bottles of liquor, flowers and plants, a few crystals, and lots of photographs of women posed shirtless on their motorcycles with their phone numbers written across their breasts. The more adventurous women show up in person, bribing their way past the security guards (I insist upon women), and often spending the night with the equipment managers (again, I insist upon women). San Francisco is no different.

There are some great local women's bands that Gloria, my childhood friend and now my manager and agent, has heard about from one of the women now backstage, a rather sultry radio DJ. Gloria wants us to check them out, although I suspect she is actually more interested in checking out the DJ. But I am lethargic, overdosed on my own ego. After a concert, I try to shake my despondency in a hot shower, try to rest my raw voice; try not to sing to Sammy.

It isn't that I never take advantage of my opportunities. I select the reticent ones, who stand off a little to the side of the fray, trying to convince themselves that they are brave. I treat them well, take them to dinner, try to talk with them. They often seem surprised that I am not stupid, that I've read a book or two. Later, I take them back to my hotel room. The sex is often mediocre; I struggle to make it scintillating. I mark them with my mouth, a bruise where I have sucked their flesh, either neck or breast. Love bites, they call them. It gives them something to remember. Occasionally, one will apologize that she is menstruating, attempting to deflect my hand from her tampon. But I will pull the string, toss the cotton cylinder, and then kiss her stomach, very gently, without any teeth at all. She will be a bit nervous when my tongue reaches her blood, but I never, never bite and soon she relaxes, letting me taste and taste. I no longer worry that this will ruin my voice; now it seems to make it stronger.

Tonight, I look around at my prospects. Among the photographs, phone numbers, and other flowers is a vase of white roses. I like the dramatic act of throwing it to the floor. The women who travel with me expect this, although they do not ask for an explanation and none is ever given. It happens every so often, some woman who could not possibly know that of all possible seductions, this is the least likely to succeed. Or sometimes I think that Gloria gets the white roses; she thinks post performance flares of energy might prevent depression.

As I grab the vase, I notice an index card hanging from a noose of white string around the thorny stems: *You've come a long way, baby. Love from the old days. Always, Sammy.*

Couldn't be, I reassure myself. There are lots of women in the world named Sammy. But are there lots of old days, lots of long ways? Still, the white roses are just coincidence. Could have been red; these were probably discounted.

I ask Gloria about the vase in my hand. She stares innocently; How would she know? she says. She was onstage with me. I ask some equipment managers. They look offended as I demean their responsibilities. I ask some security officers. They point at one another.

"I thought you'd recognize me," one security woman says. She has short, graying brown hair and red lipstick. Incredibly pale skin. Her breasts twist under the cheap fabric of her dark blue security uniform. Then she smiles her smile.

"I thought you were dead."

"I'm not," she says simply.

I wait for an explanation, looking at this ghost from an afterlife where peroxide is apparently unavailable.

"I suppose it's kind of ironic now," Sammy says. "The guys thought you weren't sexy enough."

"Because I wouldn't fuck them like you did," I say because I feel like I've earned the right to be as cruel as I want.

"No. I think it was the way you danced," she answers. "They thought you would hold the band back or something."

"What does that have to do with you being dead?" I feel like smiling at her, but I force myself not to.

"Well, if I were dead, you'd quit. Lose interest. The only reason you were in the band was to be close to me. You wanted to play the guitar as good as a guy so you'd impress me."

"I didn't quit," I protest to this ghost, this security guard, like I still care what she thinks. Then I turn on her. "Why did you go along with it?"

"I had my reasons." Her smile. I am embarrassed by how young I must have been then, how easily bruised.

She seems embarrassed too. "I came back and looked for

you," Sammy explains. "I asked your mother, but she said you were gone."

"I was," I say, but do not tell her where I went.

"Well, I just wanted to tell you how sorry I am. Real sorry."

I wonder if she lives with someone, man or woman.

"All the women I know think you're just great," Sammy continues. "Really admire you. Don't believe me when I say I knew you way back when—"

"That was a long time ago." This is pitiful. Not her, but the way I still feel drawn to her, like I want to dive into her body and rest there for eternity.

"Not so long in the scheme of things."

"I guess not," I admit.

"How about we have a drink and talk about old times?"

I think she must not be living with anyone. "I still don't drink," I answer, and then, stabbing again, "And you, still shooting up every five minutes?"

"No. Not anymore. Not since I accepted what I am."

"So, no more men?"

Sammy shrugs, changes the subject. "How's your mother?"

"Dead." Dead as I thought Sammy was. Dead as dead. But it is never my mother's face that floats from the audience while the stage is still sheathed in darkness and my fingers tense for the first chords of my trademark opening song. It has always been Sammy's pale face, its jutting white halo, its dilated pupils reflecting sequins. It has never been anything like the beige flesh that bubbles above her navy blue uniform, underneath mousy hair ridged with attempts at curls.

Looking at Sammy, I try to decide which song will open my next show, tomorrow night across the bay in Berkeley. A small, intimate club. I think I'll try something new. Perhaps something previously unrecorded; something in plaintive minor chords. A solo. There will be no time for rehearsal. My professional but still unsullied voice amplified but not distorted. My virgin Gibson semiacoustic cello guitar. Something slow and slightly sad. Like a song a lonely woman would sing to herself in the shower.

"Go get yourself two tickets for tomorrow night's show from the backstage manager," I tell Sammy. "And make sure you bring a woman as your date."

"I thought you would be my date," she says.

Same old Sammy. Confident when we sang together that her voice did not sound like shit, even though it did; and confident now that she doesn't look like shit, even though she does. Maybe it's her confidence that makes me say, "Sure." Or maybe I just wanted to see that smile. Or maybe I'm just an idiot, to pick some worn-out security guard when I could have any of the dozens of fresh young women lingering backstage.

"One ticket then." I am casual. She rewards me with her vampire smile.

It is the smile that occupies my ceiling. I can hardly sleep the next day for thinking about her. I am restless, pacing around my hotel suite, which seems too large and sunny. I take shower after shower, closing the curtain tight, creating a steamy coffin. I order room service twice. No food satisfies. I pick up my acoustic guitar, try some new arrangements, but the strings sound more eerie than any audience would tolerate.

I curse myself, curse her. Why does she reappear now? Just when everything is going great. I know I'm at the verge of breaking into the big time, beyond the women's music circuit, into the mainstream. And even if I don't, I already have a damn good career. Enough money and enough admiration. And the chance to sing and play my guitar, the only things I've ever wanted.

Or the only things I could articulate. There is something else I want. Something to satiate some emptiness at my core. I can barely tolerate the cliché, but I also can't explain the lack. Maybe it's spiritual. I've even thought of going back to the Salvation Army to sing. Have even slipped into a service or two in some depressed town or another. I've tried tarot and Rolphing and yoga and a chiropractor and every sort of sex and even, just a time or two, some heroin. And, saluting my mother, some Wild Turkey and some margaritas heavy with salt. But nothing fills the void I call Sammy.

Maybe not even she will. That's the risk of seeing her again. Oh, why the hell did I agree? I'd go take a walk, but even the ground clouds of this San Francisco evening hold too much brightness. I take another shower, sing to myself.

Finally, by twilight, Gloria comes to my room. I have dressed and undressed seventeen times. Now I'm wearing black jeans and a black ripped tee shirt. Black boots. A wide silver belt. No jewelry. Like I just threw it on three minutes ago, which I did.

"You look like death warmed over," Gloria says cheerfully. She must have had a better day than I have, must have found the DJ intriguing.

"Thanks a lot. Should I change?"

"No, it's not the outfit. That's the same. But you seem different, really. I hope you don't get that damn flu. I worry about you. All your high-risk behaviors, don't think I don't know about them. I hear things. I'm your manager, I have to know what the hell you're doing. You know, you should really get tested."

"Oh, Jesus, not now."

"Okay, okay. But are you sure you're all right?"

"Yeah," I mumble. "I'll be fine. Get me onstage."

Gloria quickly looks around my room. For a needle or a bottle or a woman or something to explain my condition. Satisfied, she directs our entourage through the streets of Berkeley to the club. She is even more satisfied when we get there. There is a line outside, pouring out of the door and down the long block, where it bubbles into a crowd at the corner. Inside, it is standing-room only, Gloria informs me, kissing me on the cheek. I look past her, to the white roses scattered on the floor, near the stage entrance. I look past her, but don't see Sammy.

Can't see her in the audience either. But I know she is there in the dark. Can feel her. Know she is not one of the women screaming, throwing her shirt onto the stage. Knows I sing only for her. And tonight, it is not my Fender that I'm fucking.

Backstage, it's over. Our drummer is still red with sweat. My voice is hoarse. Gloria is exuberant, hugging everyone.

Whispers in my ear: "Major deal. Major deal." I see some guy from the industry trailing around after her, like she trailed around after him last month.

I feel dizzy. Like I need a fix, only I'm not sure of what. Or I am sure but won't admit it. That bitch. That bitch. I don't see Sammy anywhere.

"That was great." Some reporter sidles next to me, touching my tee shirt with her hot hand. Her press badge perches on her left breast, jutting out like a bicuspid.

"She likes an intimate audience," Gloria interrupts, and then is gone again, winking.

The reporter smiles her unremarkable smile. I could have her, I think. I could bed her so easily. A slip of the tongue. A stretch of the mouth. But I can tell she would be too timid to bite hard enough. I can tell she would not be proud to be bruised. I excuse myself.

A sequined dress intercepts me. Some brutal blonde, pale and ethereal.

"That was stunning," the woman says. Then she smiles her Sammy smile.

She is the one who is stunning. And I am simply stunned. She had been standing backstage the entire time, leaning against some pole that looked like it could not support itself, never mind a human body.

"Sammy?" I half ask.

"You were expecting someone else?"

"Yes, as a matter of fact. A rather mousy-haired security guard that I met last night."

"Oh." Sammy laughs. "That was just a test."

I am suddenly angry. "What is this, the Frog and the Prince?"

"Wrong fairy tale, darling," she breathes, taking my hand. Her fingers are smooth and cool. I can only forgive her.

"Dinner? Gloria told me there's a pretty good Italian place not far from here."

"Italian? We should avoid all that garlic; we'll be happier later."

"Then you select, you live around here now."

She takes us to a Russian restaurant on College Avenue. She orders borscht, and salts it before she tastes it. I mimic her. We stir our food. We sip our vodka martinis. I have never been hungrier, less able to eat.

She drives me across Bay Bridge, back to my hotel. I don't remember having told her where it was. We sit in the bar for hours. We sip drinks that she orders. She orders more, allowing the others to be removed, virtually untouched. She walks me to my room, as if I have invited her.

I pick up my guitar. Sit on the bed. She sits next to me. My fingers caress the steel. Her finger traces my mouth. Inside my lower lip, then touching the tips of my teeth.

I am very still. Only my hands move across the body of my guitar, the neck of my guitar.

Her finger across my cheek. Behind my ear. Under my ear. Parallel with my jawbone. On my neck. Dancing.

I can hardly breathe.

"We don't have to if you don't want to."

I think that I have said this, but then it seems she is waiting for an answer as if she has.

"I want—"

She closes the hotel room drapes. The first flickers of dawn, the last lights of the city, all erased.

I reach for her sequins across the darkness. The single zipper. The music of it is like sex itself, both secretive and simple. I smell her thickness. She smells the same as she always has.

But not everything is the same. She was once the one who reached for me. Her kisses were sloppy then, her motions jagged. And I was more compliant. Without the confidence to take what I wanted, who I wanted and how. Without the audacity to pretend I knew. No, not everything is the same.

I feel her strain against her passivity. I push my knee between hers, then up, higher, until I hit the bone, where it feels like all the solids are seeping out. Some sticky wet spreads through the leg of my jeans. I wonder vaguely if she is menstruating; that must be the thickness I smell. I long to taste it, to drink it, to have it stiffen on my cheeks. Soon, I promise myself, knowing I must go slow so that I do not startle her, knowing I must do nothing that will make her change her mind about giving me this gift. About coming back.

But she is already moving beyond me. Against my leg, wet and chafing, under and over. The sound in my ear is a howl, but whispered. It cannot be misunderstood. She is only calm for a moment, her sounds still reverberating, when her mouth is on my earlobe, then lower. Her teeth catch my flesh. My skin swirls between her lips until my whole body is caught in some whirlpool. My own teeth bang against each other, lonely in their shaking.

The word *orgasm* appears on the edges of my consciousness casting for an explanation, but then quickly recedes, embarrassed by its paucity. This must be something different. Less like falling and more like ascending; less like death and more like being born.

By the time I wake, I've lost a day. I'm still fully clothed. I expect to see Sammy sitting in my room, somewhere. Instead, it is Gloria.

"We've been worried about you, kid."

"I'm fine." I rush to the bathroom, greedy for the mirror. I look for one of Sammy's notorious love bites, but my skin glimmers, translucent and unbroken.

Terrified that it has all been a fever, I search the room. The hotel sheets are certainly a bloody mess. The silver-sequined dress is spread on the night table, over the phone. I slip into it, not surprised that it fits.

"It's you," Gloria exclaims. "You can wear it on TV. I got you a spot on a music awards special!"

It isn't the promise of some transitory fame that makes me smile. It's Sammy.

pas de deux

entrée

Once inside the room, nothing on the other side of its mirrored walls matters. Not the family member with last night's
liquor still puddled on the wisdom teeth. Not the sour smell
of damp papers by the stained kitchen sink. Not the broken
glass of the sky. Not the hammered past or the crack of the
future. Nothing.

What matters inside the room of worn wooden floors
is only what is inside the room. What matters is this: the hips
turned out, the fingers floating, the arms like wings, and the
legs like wire. The foot like a cup that could hold the finest
wine. What matters is the high leap. The thighs split wide, parallel to the ceiling. A word called out, a command: higher. Or
wider. Or more control. What is important is that the face be
kept expressionless. Unless a specific expression is required.

adagio

Madame uses a stick for correction. It is not thick, but slender,
like a long cigarette holder. Sometimes she holds it like that, as

if she will bring it to her lips and suck on it. But most of the time she grips it loosely as she paces; she could be a horse trainer if she were dressed differently.

The stick can be used as a compliment. In Madame's hand, it can trace the line of leg like a caress. It can interlace the fingers, coaxing the bones to be more liquid. It can huddle behind the knee, a baby asleep in its mother's competent arms.

At the barre—four, five, six—the seventh in a series of sixteen battement tendus from fifth position. The black lacquer stick strikes the corner of my lips, stinging. Madame Karmakov puts the index finger of her other hand, the hand without the stick, to her own lips. I must have been counting again, moving my mouth, kissing each number into the room.

Giselle giggles, turns around to advise, *"Fermez la bouche."* Her own battement tendu is sloppy, her toes leaving the floor far too soon, her return to fifth position imprecise. She earns no correction from Madame. The corner of my lip throbs with this injustice.

I want to do everything perfect for Madame. I want to be her favorite, her pet, her protégé. I want to be the one who softens the sharp sapphire blue of her eyes. I want the cigarette holder of her stick to burn a compliment onto my thigh.

Even if Madame were to strike Giselle's partially turned-out leg, Giselle would probably not even feel it. Over her tights, Giselle wears latex pants that squeak as she moves. She says these help keep her muscles warm, but I know she is trying to lose weight by sweating it away. She'd probably have more success if she gave up the bags of potato chips and chocolate chip cookies that she tries to hide under her bed. If I were really Madame's pet, perhaps I would tattle on my roommate, Giselle. But that is not the kind of pet I want to be.

Though perhaps that is better than not being a pet at all. According to Giselle, I will never be a favorite. First, there is my hair: blond, tinged with red during those rare times it is subjected to direct sunlight. But adding to this injury are my freckles, splashed across my nose like insults. There has never been a ballerina with freckles. Of this, Giselle is absolutely certain and tells me so. Repeatedly. As she eats another chocolate chip cookie sandwiched between two potato chips.

In the small room we share, I hammer at my toe shoes while Giselle crunches. I am trying to soften the toes, to break the box meant to protect the tender toes as they strain to support the body. But the box can never be a safeguard, only strength in the toes and the instep can prevent injury, at least according to the wisdom of the prima ballerinas. As I assault the black satin of my shoes, I imagine myself Pavlova, hammering away like she did, perfecting her pastel-pink points.

I learned about Pavlova's elegant hammering while doing a composition for Madame Karmakov, who makes us write reports about famous ballerinas. I think I may be the only one who actually does the weekly assignment. It was Giselle who figured out that all we needed to do was have the ballerina's name at the top and a few of the names of the ballets for which she was most famous on the page. The rest of the words could be nonsense. Madame K. could not read English.

She can hardly speak it either. Sometimes it seems as if her entire English vocabulary consists of the words *yes, no,* and *nice.* Though she combines these words into evocative phrases such as "no nice." But Madame K. doesn't really need English. She has a vocabulary entire in her black stick.

And she has the vocabulary of ballet itself. Her arm saying port de bras. Her foot pronouncing frappé. Which are words she also knows, of course, the French gliding from her mouth in its satin slipper of Russian.

Once I asked Madame K. if what we were studying was classical Russian ballet, why all the words were in French.

"No nice," she said, tapping my derriere with her black lacquer stick.

I thought I saw a flash of humor, but faster than lightning, it was gone from the sky of her eyes.

I eventually did a report on Madame herself. Katrinka Karmakov. Born in St. Petersburg, entered into the Imperial Ballet at the age of twelve, was a member of the Maryinski Theatre until 1917, when she left for Paris, eventually becoming a ballerina with Diaghilev's Ballet Russe. Leaving Paris in 1938 for the U.S., becoming a teacher at a famous New York City academy. Our own Northeastern Academy of Ballet is not mentioned. Her principle roles were Naïla in *La Source*, Odette-Odile in *Swan Lake*, and Giselle in *Giselle*.

Perhaps I could change my name from Nathalie to Naïla.

Though Madame always calls me Natasha.

I imagined my own entry in the encyclopedia. Naïla? Natasha? Natalie? Nathalie? But under whichever name, I want my sketch to be exactly the same length as Madame's. Which is certainly not as long as the one for Pavlova. Or for the famous teacher Agrippina Vagarnova. Or for my American favorite, Maria Tallchief, who I pretend is not only an American Indian but has constellations of freckles. Madame's entry is brief. And there is no photograph.

She returns the report to me without comment. Not even her usual "nice."

Though perhaps seeing Giselle mentioned as one of her principle roles gives her the idea to mount it as our spring ballet, the performance terminating the academic year. The one that parents come to see. And perhaps even some of Madame's friends from professional ballets, offering the best students places in the better schools, the ones associated with real companies.

My roommate, Giselle, is thrilled when word drifts through the academy that *Giselle* will be our spring performance. She announces to everyone that she will be the prima ballerina. Why else would Madame choose *Giselle* as the ballet, Giselle poses her rhetorical question, posing her left leg in an arabesque of squeaky latex behind her. She wobbles.

I think she will need practice before she can perform the ballet, especially the famous pas de deux. The entrée demands only some style, but the adagio section with the arabesques will be difficult. The variations in solo are not simple, especially for a dancer like Giselle, whose thick legs do not allow the leaps required. And then the last section, the coda, requiring both the posing controls and the leaps—I do not think she is quick enough. Or thoughtful enough.

But I keep my opinions, my jealousies, my criticism of Madame's poor judgment, to myself. As I hold close my secret lust to be Queen of the Wilis. The Queen character in *Giselle*, I decide, is actually more interesting than Giselle herself. Yes, she is a solo part and not a part for a prima ballerina, but the Queen, after all, is a queen. Even if she is dead. She is ethereal. She is the commander of all the others who have died before consummating their love. I am not exactly sure what this means, though I think it must mean she is blond, though probably lacking in freckles.

I will practice my leaps until they are executed so slowly that I seem to float. I will wear pink toe shoes instead of my usual black. At first everyone mocked my black shoes, with their hammered toes so that they always looked old. But Madame herself had pointed her stick at my arch when I was en pointe and said "Yes, nice, Odile," and almost smiled. I could perform Odile, the Black Swan in *Swan Lake*, someday. That's what Madame must have been saying. I think of this as I pound my toe shoes harder, knowing the Black Swan is the double of the white swan queen, imagining myself as I dance. My leaps are pure, like birds in flight. I wish Madame had chosen *Swan Lake* instead of *Giselle* as the spring ballet. But that wish is worthless; I will not waste my wishing on something that has already been decided. I hammer the side of my shoe, each strike a prayer that I will be chosen for a different queen. Queen of the Wilis.

But when the list is posted, I am not Queen of the Wilis.

Instead, I am named as Giselle.

I hear it before I see it. From Giselle herself. Who is yelling and cursing as she pulls her plastic pants away from her legs, squeaking with sweat.

"You're her pet," Giselle accuses me. We are in our small room and she is standing between me and the door. I sidle around her as best I can, but she shoves me. Still, I escape. And sit in the reading room, looking up the famous ballerinas who have performed Giselle.

When I return to our room, Giselle is not there. My pointe shoes are on my bed, filled with smashed snacks. The crumbs of the potato chips cling to the black satin like salty little stars. This could have happened to Pavlova, I console myself. I am lucky it's chocolate chips. In Russia, I've read, they used ground glass. Very effective when secreted in the toe shoe of a competitor.

At the end of Madame's pointe class, unusual only because of Giselle's absence and my grease-smudged shoes, I wait my turn to perform the révérence and exit. I love the révérence, that ballet-modified curtsy a student gives the teacher to thank her for the class. My demi-plié is a little deeper than usual. I want to express my gratitude to Madame for assigning me the role, but more for her confidence that I can do it. I also want to see some indication of pleasure in her own blue eyes. But she is, as usual, unreadable.

I stay to practice at the barre. My glissade must be infused with tragedy. It must tell of my love for the devious Albrecht. I must have a jeté that conveys my madness at his betrayal. And my arabesque must show how I will forgive Albrecht, saving him from the Queen of the Wilis, who would condemn him to certain death. Glissade. Glissade. Jeté. Jeté. Arabesque. The barre is Albrecht, my partner in the pas de deux.

The next class is beginning, evicting me from my home with the worn wooden floors, but as I try to slip away, I am caught on the tenterhook of my name: Nathalie, accented in a false French. I see Giselle's mother gesticulating to Madame in the hallway outside the room. Giselle's mother was a prima ballerina. And not just any prima ballerina. One of the ones some weird but famous artist who made shadow boxes of ballerinas used as a model. Or that's what Giselle tells me. Repeatedly. Like I know about shadow boxes and artists. Though her mother looks the part, in that stereotyped way. With the erect carriage and the dark hair pulled severely away from her face. And the sense of entitlement, extending to her daughter.

So unlike my own mother, who had little interest in dancing or in me. I started lessons as a child because that's what happened to little girls on the Upper West Side of Manhattan in 1964. And what happened to their mothers in the next several years was something the women called "the movement" and the men called "women's lib." It sent my mother back to Barnard, and eventually into graduate school, where she is now, writing a dissertation on some woman writer called Carson McCullers.

It sent my father to the bars, gradually altering his career goal from famous attorney to alcoholic.

And it sent me to Pennsylvania. To the Northeastern Academy of Ballet.

"You like to dance," my mother concluded, and sent me off to a boarding school that specialized in pirouettes and anorexia. My father's family paid the tuition.

Madame seems to shrink besides Giselle's mother. I can hear her soft voice. "Yes. Yes."

Giselle's mother is not in the *Encyclopedia of Ballet*. I looked. I asked Giselle her mother's name, just to make sure. She must have been a dancer—for who else would name a daughter Giselle?—but she is not a ballerina who deserves an entry in any encyclopedia. There are no ballet students writing reports about her.

I hear Giselle's mother arguing that Nathalie's coloring is incorrect. She is pointing out that Giselle, my roommate—like the famous ballerinas who had danced Giselle, like Madame herself, and so, somehow, like the ballet character Giselle—has dark hair. Vital for the mad scene, Giselle's mother contends, touching her own French twist.

Madame nods, as if in agreement.

"Look in her room," Giselle's mother instructs. "Cookies and snacks that she tried to force my little Giselle to consume. Potato chips, if you can believe that. She is no ballerina."

Madame says, "Yes, yes, yes," to Giselle's mother.

But with Madame, this could mean anything.

I hold my breath, waiting, seemingly for days. Nothing changes.

Except that Giselle is gone.

Except that I meet with the director of the academy. I had thought it was Madame's school. I only understood things were different when I met with a wizened old man I had thought was the janitor or maybe an old balletmaster long past his prime who was allowed to hang out at the academy. He keeps asking me the same questions, as if repetition might alleviate his German-sounding accent or provoke a different answer. He asks me whether Madame had ever been "untoward" and whether she had ever touched me "inappropriatewise." Throughout the interview, I think of Madame's stick, especially the times it had stung my mouth, but I do not consider tattling. I deserved every correction, but know that Herr Director might not agree. So, I keep my guilty mouth shut.

Preparing for *Giselle*.

At the barre, asleep, reading the encyclopedia, banging my toe shoes, I am everywhere and always preparing for *Giselle*.

Jeté, jeté, balloté, balloté. I dance with the entire corps de ballet. I am a peasant, like Giselle. But a special peasant, as my solo demonstrates, my near-perfect glissade, then piqué, an arabesque. The romantic mad scene, my sunny hair tumbling from its French twist, the strategic pin I pull from my hair working its magic as Madame had demonstrated. I whirl in arabesque, without wobbling. My slow développé, on flat foot. Then into arabesque, promenade around the stage, entrechat six, and around to one long arabesque.

There is applause.

I had forgotten the audience. The performance. I smell the old wood floor of the practice room. I am in a black leotard and my black toe shoes, although everyone else sees the costume I am wearing.

The youngest member of the corps approaches me with a bouquet. I know what to do; I know the traditions. But when I pluck a single red rose from the spray for my prince, I cannot extend my arm toward the pimply boy dancing Albrecht who partnered me adequately in the pas de deux. Instead, I walk to the wings and pull Madame onto the stage. With a révérence, I kiss the rose and extend it to her.

For I must have read somewhere that the most important pas de deux is between the ballerina and her teacher.

variations: solo

My students are not hungry; they are not the kind of girls who starve themselves for art. I find them complacent, even when talented. I try to remind myself that I really have no idea what my students truly feel, I only know what they perform. But the lack of striving to correct a sickled foot must evince a lack of passion. What else could it mean?

Donna has the possibility of being different. There is a seriousness about her, a substance to her révérence at the end of class. I have been told that my insistence on the révérence is old-fashioned. I have replied that all of classical ballet is old-fashioned. I have smiled. I have thought: That is how Madame Karmakov taught me and that is how I, Madame Natasha, will teach my students.

Every révérence from one of my students is a révérence to her.

After my performance of *Giselle*, and my red rose révérence to Madame Karmakov, she came to the tiny backstage dressing area where I was removing my toe shoes. I stood up because I thought she was going to hug me, but she simply handed me an envelope and walked away. I don't know what I thought it was, but by the time I figured out it was a letter of introduction (written in Russian) to those who would be my new teachers, I was back home in New York and Madame had vanished from the Northeastern Academy of Ballet.

I was asked not to come back, although I would not have gone even if they had begged me. I would not go back there after what they had done to Madame.

Though I wasn't exactly sure what they had done. Fired her? Made her angry enough to quit? Somehow it involved me, I knew, me and *Giselle* and Giselle. And Giselle's mother. It was my mother who used the term "lesbian-baiting." She had learned it at one of her consciousness-raising sessions, which is where she was when she wasn't at the library or at some meeting. "The same thing happened to her." By "her" my mother always meant Carson McCullers, the subject of the never-ending dissertation. I asked my mother to do something, to find out where Madame had gone. But my mother was too busy. And I wound up at another dance academy, this one in Washington, D.C. My father's family did not have to pay; I auditioned and was awarded a scholarship. I did not give them Madame's letter.

I danced and danced and danced and didn't eat. Not cookies, not potato chips. Only grapefruit. Some bread. A bit of rice.

And then I became a professional.

Of sorts.

I floated from company to company, from teacher to teacher. No one was like Madame. No one carried a black lacquer stick. No one made her students do silly reports on famous ballerinas, or even made us read, or even cared if the dancers knew the story of the ballet we were supposed to be dancing. It was all technique. A bottle of aspirin for the tendinitis. No surgery for the bunions, which gave a nice line to the foot anyway, like wings.

I heard she was in St. Petersburg.

I took a demotion to dance in the corps of a company because it was scheduled to tour the Soviet Union. I looked for her everywhere in what was now named Leningrad. I hunted down elderly ballerinas and asked about Katrinka Karmakov. Some had known her, but no one knew where she was now.

I joined another company. Then another. I lived in Salt Lake City, in San Francisco, in Minneapolis. When the choreography called for a jumper, my name would be posted. I could earn the applause of those members of the audience stupid enough to be impressed with pyrotechnics, the ones who studiously counted the fouettés of the Swan Queen in *Swan Lake*, feeling superior if the ballerina accomplished only thirty-one instead of the required thirty-two. But though I could do the thirty-two, could do fifty-two—I never danced the Swan Queen, never danced Odile in the black toe shoes I still favored for practice. Never danced Giselle again, though I often danced a Wili; not Queen of the Wilis, but merely a Wili, a dead spirit of a girl who had died before consummating her love.

It was my favorite part.

The only part I could practice with the requisite ambition, when I could infuse every port de bras with lust.

Some days, lifting my leg at the barre and practicing a slow développé, I thought my mother was wrong. I decided Madame's departure was simply another incident in the intriguing world of ballet. I blamed Giselle's mother and the power she wielded as a passé ballerina twirling around a small town in Pennsylvania.

Other days, I thought my mother must have been correct. That there must have been some threat, some bludgeon. There must have been an element in the story of the ballet that was invisible, but that explains everything: the never-apparent knife that Giselle stabs herself with as the cause of her death. My unconsummated love for Madame must have been that dangerous.

In every city, I thought about going to a gay bar, but first I was too young and then I was too old. Though the real problem was that I was scared. Not scared of the usual things, like being thought queer, but scared to go into a bar, any bar. I told myself that I didn't have anything to wear; I couldn't very well pirouette across the floor in a black leotard and pink tights and black en pointe shoes, could I? Even with a ballet skirt. The truth was I was scared when I was anywhere other than the room. With its comforting wood floors and its ballet barre. Even the stage was becoming frightening, but I managed there, thinking of it as the payment I had to make to get back into the room. I scheduled six hours of classes a day, every day.

I leaped at the first offer to teach that came my way. Not exactly my way, but the way of the company of which I was nominally part. We were touring there and the academy owner came to the performance and even put up a sign. Looking for someone to teach classical. To teach Russian.

We were in St. Petersburg.

The one in Florida.

The balletmaster gave me a wonderful reference. The owner of the academy, Rosa Weibert, mentioned my performance as Queen of the Wilis instead of some nondescript Wili. I didn't correct her mistake. She told me she had been a Rockette. I angled my head as if I possessed the neck of a swan, in a way I hoped was complimentary but noncommittal. I got the job.

I learned to like it here. Especially the wide flat streets, like stages almost. Unlike the raked stages of Russia, slanted so that a jeté toward the audience gives the illusion of even more height. I do my barre work near dawn every day at the academy, in the room with the worn wooden floors and the never-clean mirrors. Then I walk on the beach, my blond hair turned blonder, my skin finally tan, the freckles blending together into a smooth brown. My mother comes down for a week in the winter, staying at the famous Don Caesar Hotel, a massive pink construction on the beach. She's in public relations now, never having finished her dissertation. My sober-for-six-years father telephones me once a month. He has a new wife and three new daughters and they all live someplace in California. "Are you eating all right?" he always asks. "Yes," I always answer. Wondering if he thinks it was me with the cookies under my bed. Or what he recalls from those days, if he can recall anything.

The Beach Academy of Dance is just a little building in a strip mall, not far from the beach. Day students only. Lessons in classical ballet, toe, tap, modern dance, and something called adult fitness. We share the mall with a veterinarian and with a doughnut shop, where the mothers sit and sip coffee while waiting for their daughters' lessons to be over. The lessons are only an hour, not an hour and a half, and this isn't the only compromise.

I do not carry a stick.

I never touch them.

My English is perfect. And my French pronunciations passable, though still hammered soft with Russian.

"Turn out from the hips, then glissade," I tell Donna. She has reddish hair folded into a bun, long limbs, and a gap between her two front teeth that her family should remedy. It ruins her smile, which is too broad anyway. It stains her face when she has accomplished a difficult combination.

Still, she is my favorite student.

She's a leaper, as I was. A track and field star en pointe. She will make a fine Giselle in the spring recital of the Beach Academy of Dance.

After I announced Giselle to the students, telling them the story of it and naming the great dancers who had performed it, including the great Madame Katrinka Karmakov, Rosa Weibert calls me into her small office. If the recital had to be classical ballet—she emphasized every syllable of the word *classical*— *Swan Lake* would be better, wouldn't it? More people know it, don't they? And we did it last year, didn't we? Though, of course, something contemporary is even better. Perhaps *Rhapsody in Blue*. Or *West Side Story*.

Her repertoire seems to have been frozen at 1964.

Or before.

And she seems to have forgotten what she had hired me to teach.

"And remember," she adds, "this year needs to be shorter. The fathers don't have a very long attention span, do they?"

I suggest *Giselle's Revenge,* a ballet satire in which Giselle lures the unsuspecting Albrecht into her coffin and then nails him into it, all the while screaming with blood-curdling glee.

Rosa Weibert shakes her head so that her hair bounces from side to side.

"Well, I suppose *Giselle* will be fine. Gigi will be good in the lead. And we can put a synopsis in the program."

"Gigi? She's not the best student."

"Oh, but she is."

"Not for this part."

"She will be." Rosa Weibert, the woman who pays my salary and therefore pays my rent, the former Rockette, the owner of the Beach Academy of Ballet, could not be more definite. There is nothing to discuss.

At least not between us.

In my own head, however, the conversation is passionate. Much of it is not in English, or even in words. There is the correction of the stick. There is an arabesque and chocolate chip cookies crushed into my black toe shoes. There is the perfect glissade. There is my mother's raw voice: "lesbian-baiting." And my father, driving us back home after my performance in *Giselle*, more drunk than I had ever seen him before. Madame says only, "No nice," but her eyes glint accusingly blue from everyone else's face.

Though it's true that Gigi has the coloring for the part, if not the extension. And the background. Lessons since she was three, three times a week. She's been en pointe the longest, certainly, before I arrived at the academy. Though she probably started too early, injuring her bones. And she knows how to elongate her spine. And she does have the necessary family support: Her mother never joins the others at the doughnut shop, but sits in the waiting room during every class, having lost the desperate war she waged to move a bench into the classroom and observe.

"Gigi. Pay attention to your feet, not your audience." Gigi has been looking in the mirror, admiring herself or perhaps seeking the admiration of her mother through the wall.

Gigi giggles.

"Ballet is not a joke," I scold. "You have to like it better than being loved."

"But it is being loved, isn't it, Madame Natasha." Donna has intruded, whether to protect Gigi or upstage her, it's difficult to decide.

"No. It is not. The audience does not really love you. No matter the applause."

"Not the audience, Madame Natasha." Donna looks down at her pointe shoes. "Just the doing."

"The doing is the doing," I answer.

"Doing it right. You know, like you always say. The perfect frappé. And it's like the perfect frappé is being loved."

I nod my head in agreement, not wanting to tell her how wrong she is. And how right.

Her frappés as Queen of the Wilis on performance night are not perfect, but they are much better than anything being done by Gigi as Giselle.

Giselle's battement tendu is sloppy, her toes leaving the floor far too soon, her return to fifth position imprecise. Her toe shoes sound like tap toes, *clunk-clunk-clunk* across the polished wood floor of the stage. Her arabesque wobbles.

Madame would never forgive me.

But I am ready to forgive Gigi when it is all over and she is standing on the stage with her bouquet of red roses and she takes one out and rather than give it to the boy performing Albrecht, she walks across the stage toward me, her Madame, her teacher.

I stand perfectly still.

Ready to accept the rose. To walk out on the stage, looking out into the audience of parents and grandparents of my students, not a ballet scout in sight, and accept Gigi's révérence, and do my own, looking as if it is back to her and to all the other dancers, but really directing it toward my own Madame.

I stand perfectly still.

Ready to accept every accolade. My foot does not move toward Gigi, my student. I correct my posture, knowing that soon everyone will be looking at me. Me, the teacher.

My face struggles to remain expressionless.

Even as she rumbles past me, past her one and only Madame, into the wing where her mother has lifted herself from out of the audience, where she belongs. Holding her mother's hand and pulling her out onto the stage. Giving her mother—her mother!—the rose that is meant only for her Madame.

Donna, Queen of the Wilis, looks across the stage at me with her sharp blue eyes, flashing her ugliest gap-toothed grin.

coda

Making love is like dancing. Only a few basic positions and all else is innovation. Derivation. Some intermediation. Reversals. And like dancing, with repetition comes perfection.

Only after hundreds of glissades can a dancer make the glissade say something other than gliding. Something other than demi-plié in fifth position, slide front pointed right foot into second position, demi-plié again, slide back pointed left foot into fifth position. Something other than preparation for a leap.

Only after hundreds can the glissade communicate passion or love or betrayal or hope. Only after hundreds can the dancer make the glissade her own. Inflect it with her own interpretation. Add it to her vocabulary.

And so it seems the same with a hand on a lover's breast.

It takes hundreds of attempts.

I have touched her breast hundreds of times. Fluttered her nipple between my fingers. Bent my mouth and sipped as if her flesh were marble fountains. Slid my hands into the river that rushed between her legs.

And my movements are finally my own. I had been taught some of them by others, and some by her, and some I had known so long they seem simply natural. But now each is my own. Even the absolute stillness required at times when partnering. I could now express any piece of the universe in my immobility.

She likes to talk. And with her I have learned to use words, to tell her the story of a ballet called *Giselle* without a single step en pointe, without a single glissade or port de bras. She taught me to speak of my parents, to mention my mother's attention to Carson McCullers with humor sometimes and with bitterness other times, to talk of my father without my own throat burning with liquor.

I even spoke of Madame, though I never thought I conveyed what I felt. My words were too imprecisely executed. I waited for the correction at the place my lips still met each other.

But my words about Madame must have been successful somehow. For one night, she surprised me during our lovemaking. We were both naked, sweat forming a little lake between my breasts in the Florida humidity, when she told me to wait a moment. In our small bathroom—smaller than most dressing rooms in Russia—she is noisy. I hear the door creak open and do not hear that the toilet has been flushed.

And she is standing there, at the bottom of our bed, my lover, Marina. In our house, the one we are buying. Our beautiful dilapidated home with the worn wooden floors. Complete with a second bedroom, hung with my favorite pair of hammered black toe shoes and equipped with a barre and one mirrored wall. The house in a part of the city known as Gulfport to the cartographers and Dykeport to some of its residents. They say that relationships begun in bars don't last, but we must be an exception.

I met her in the bar, on a usual night, on a night I could have met anyone else, on a night just like other nights that I had met other women. I was wearing a black leotard and a pair of cutoffs and black ballet slippers and was playing pool with a woman I had met on another night. I was thinking of going home with this woman again, depending upon whether or not I could beat her at the game we were now shooting.

I wish I could say that I began going to the bar the night of the *Giselle* recital, the very night that Gigi failed to give révérence to me and to Madame, the night that Donna mocked my every failure with her gap-toothed smile. I imagine myself in the bar that night, drinking vodka on the rocks, the melting ice glittering like ground glass. And maybe the first time I told Marina the story, that was my interpretation.

But that's not precise.

That's so sloppy that it's false.

Sometimes one sees the lightning but can't react until after the thunder comes. I've learned that here, in St. Petersburg, the thunderstorm capital of the world. Sometimes even after the thunder, it's best to wait.

So I waited.

I didn't storm out. I didn't write my favorite student a letter of reference in another language and disappear. No, I continued teaching her. Her and the other, less talented ones. I danced that summer in a ballet in Sarasota. *Swan Lake.*

I went to classes.

Not only ballet classes, but classes at the community college. Going to the career counselor. What do you suggest for a has-been, second-rate ballerina? I obtained a certificate in geriatric physical education.

St. Petersburg is what the world will soon look like. Old people everywhere. Marina disagrees, but she is a dog groomer.

"Don't you notice your customers?" I ask her.

"My customers are the dogs. Some are old and some are young and most are in the middle."

"How about the ones who tell you what to do?" I tease.

"Bath. Flea dip. Cut in a certain style."

"I listen to the dogs," she says. "No matter what a person wants, it's the dog that decides. A swirl of fur can say everything."

"And do they pay you?" I am still trying to provoke her.

"In a way," she says solemnly.

But even if Marina doesn't notice them, the people in this city constitute the aged. Some of them seem as ancient as ballet. White hair and yellow fingernails and speaking languages I've never heard. Though I recognize the Russians, of course. The oldest émigrés mumble about "the revolution" as if it happened yesterday.

I ask some of the oldest women: Did you study at the Imperial Ballet? Did you dance with the Maryinski Theatre? With Diaghilev's Ballet Russe? Were your principals roles in Naïla in *La Source*, Odette-Odile in *Swan Lake*, and Giselle in *Giselle*? Did you ever have a favorite student named Natasha?

I ask them this without saying a word.

I wait for their answers.

As I am waiting now.

Waiting for my feelings to coalesce into a language with words. Waiting, as I look at Marina, standing at the foot of our bed, wearing one of my leotards that binds her breasts and brandishing what looks like a riding crop and smoking a cigarette.

And I understand what she is telling me. That she will be Madame for me. That I can abandon my role as a Wili, queen of unconsummated love. That I can finally have what I've wanted, or at least the fantasy version of it. That our bed will become the room with no need for mirrors because we will be able to see ourselves with clarity, even as we will have no need to look. That we can perform the jubilant coda of our pas de deux; that the ballet of our struggle for happiness will not be a tragedy. That love prevails.

And although I understand every nuance of her language, I start to laugh.

Maybe it's the boots.

"Well, your toe shoes didn't fit me," she says. "I got them down from the wall and tried. I couldn't even walk in them."

"But cowboy boots?" I can't stop giggling.

"Well, they do have pointy toes." Marina tries to pout.

"Baby," I say, "take off your outfit and come to bed."

"Nathalie," she says, "I mean, Natasha, don't you think I'm sexy?" She turns her feet out into an attempt at second position, her hips staying behind.

"I think Marina is sexy," I say.

When she is naked, I pull her down onto our bed, and it's a ballet. Though a comic one, since I keep flouncing into laughter.

Laughter sneaks up on me the entire next day, as I stand in a room with worn wooden floors, looking at the elderly students in my advanced "Movement for Seniors" class. It's really just a few steps, some sliding and bending and stretching. I insisted on the installation of barres in all the practice rooms and make my students use them for balance. The students hold tight to the barres and try to look at the mirrors to see themselves.

I make them count out loud.

In English.

"Stretch to the front," I say. "Again. Again. Four. Five. Six. To the back. Again. Again. Four. Five. Six."

Some try to point their toes in their sneakers. Some wear slippers. Bedroom slippers, not ballet slippers. She always stays a few moments after class. Looking for a bit of extra attention. Wanting to be the favorite.

"Yes, nice?" she asks, pointing her toes in front of her, a battement tendu from a nicely turned out first position. I admire the elderly arch. Her blue eyes are watery, crepuscular. She wobbles into a curtsy.

"Yes, nice." I laugh, returning a revérénce. Realizing I have finally stopped looking for Madame. Finding her everywhere.

Close to Utopia

The Utopians wonder that any mortal takes pleasure in the uncertain sparkle of a tiny jewel or precious stone when he can look at a star or even the sun itself . . .

When nature bids you to be good to others, she does not command you conversely to be cruel and merciless to yourself. So nature herself, they maintain, prescribes to us a joyous life or, in other words, pleasure . . .

—*Saint Thomas More, in* **Utopia,** *1516*

PART ONE: JOY

*T*he kitchen floor is my sky. The blue linoleum is that same color as two minutes before twilight, or three minutes after dawn. Even the speckles of shiny silver embedded in the floor look like they might be stars, or the seeds of clouds. If I lay my face down on the cool linoleum and squint my eyes, it can almost seem like I'm back where I belong, standing in the wide front yard and letting the whole world swallow me.

It can almost seem like I am happy again. Though I was just a kid then, so maybe I wasn't really happy, just too stupid to know any different. Mom says things are better now, that an apartment is better than any trailer; that the city is better than the country; that the North is better than the South. Mom says it doesn't matter that we don't have a yard anymore. No one has a yard here, or at least what seems like a yard to me. A piece of ground no bigger than a grave is not a yard.

I tried to tell Marisa this. About the size of the yard and a grave, but she didn't seem to care. That's Marisa, always trying to seem like she doesn't care. But she does. I know she does. I know it because one day we were sharing a cigarette. It was cold, so cold that my ears were burning. Which is another thing that I don't like about it here. It's cold for a long, long time and the few scrawny trees lose any leaves they had and it's so ugly that it's hard to believe it's not a nightmare. But people just walk around like it's normal. The way I walked around after Marisa and the cigarette and the kiss. Normal.

When spring comes, everybody acts real happy. Like someone has stopped beating them up. Like the world might be alive after all. Like it's really special that there's a pathetic little bud on some mangled tree. Like it's a damn miracle—which it is.

And then the bud turns into some sort of bloom and then it drops off and then it's almost summer, like now. And it's hot as hell.

It's hotter here than it ever was in Florida. Where there was a breeze, off the ocean or around the lake or across the Glades. And we had a yard. No matter where we lived, in whatever part of the state my mother found a job or a man, we always had a yard. A yard bigger than a grave.

I think the sky is what I miss most. I would like to show Marisa the sky, the way it spreads huge into a thousand different shades of blue. The way it borders itself with purple. Or explodes into orange. She would care then; a sky like that is enough to make anybody care. But I can't. Not just because I don't get to go outside or see Marisa much anymore. Even when I was outside and was sharing a cigarette with Marisa, even on the best of days, the sky seemed all crowded with brick. The buildings aren't really that high—not skyscrapers like in Manhattan—but I guess it is because they are so close together that there is only an alley of light.

So in some ways, it's better to stay inside. Better to stay here, looking at the kitchen floor, waiting for two minutes after twilight when my mother will be back from work and might bring me some Chinese food from my favorite place around the corner, right on Utopia Parkway. Better to stay here, my left ankle in a handcuff, chained to the radiator pipe.

*T*he kitchen floor is my ocean. The blue linoleum rolls from corner to corner like the calmest of seas, rough only near the dirty cloud that is the stove. Even the shimmering flecks impressed in a random pattern on the floor look like they might be foam, a promise of unbroken whitecaps. If I lay my head back on the hot afternoon floor and close my eyes, it can almost seem like I'm back where I belong, spread on the hot sand of a real beach and letting the sun bake all the evil out of me.

Happy on a real beach. Like the ones near Fort Pierce, where we lived when my mother took up with that crew leader who had the red truck. Or even like the ones on the other side of Florida, the Gulf side, where the water was calm but very aqua and the sand was pink with crushed coquina shells. Not like the beach that Marisa took me to. I must have been telling her how much I missed the ocean when she suggested we cut school and go to Rockaway Beach. She said it wasn't really that far: "If we had a car, we could just jump on the BQE." I pretended as if I knew what the BQE was, later figuring out it was a highway called the Brooklyn Queens Expressway. I pretended as if it was just a minor annoyance that we didn't have a car, not saying that even if we did, neither of us was old enough to drive. Though I was thinking that Marisa was old enough to drive in Florida, where everything, including kids, could grow faster.

We sat on subways for hours. First into Manhattan and then out again into Brooklyn, a big semicircle on the subway map. Apparently, there was no subway under the BQE. That's the thing I don't understand about it here. Or one of the things. It's like they don't want the people with cars above the ground and the people who ride subways underneath the ground to be on the same paths. Maybe the earth would collapse. Though I still think it would make more sense if the routes at least ran in the same directions. Like 95 and A1A—running north/south along the Atlantic Ocean. Or Alligator Alley and Heavenly Seventy—running east/west, below or above Lake Okeechobee. But here, everything is crowded into a maze and there are a million ways to get from one place to the next and a billion ways to get lost.

It was still cold when we got there. Although it was May and way past spring. I pulled my shirt around me and started to complain.

Marisa had no pity for me. "Of course it's cold. The frost date isn't till the fifteenth," she said.

"How do you know about frost dates?" I was surprised. Frost dates are things that farm workers know, not girls from Queens. I smiled to imagine Marisa in an orange grove in north Florida, swinging a smudge pot to keep the fruit from freezing.

"My grandfather has a fig tree in the yard."

I tried to remember if figs were tropical, but all I knew about them was that their leaves could be posed on naked people like Adam and Eve and Greek statutes. But those naked people must be from warm places; they're never wearing parkas or shivering.

"You can grow figs way up here?" I fished for information.

"My grandfather can."

"Any oranges? Avocados?" For a moment it seemed as if anything was possible. As if Marisa's grandfather could have found some secret.

"No, just a fig tree."

"Mangoes?"

"No."

"How about bananas? I had a banana tree once, but the bananas were tiny."

"No. I'm telling you he just grows figs. Just figs. Jesus Christ, Joy Parker."

Whenever Marisa gets annoyed at me that's what she says: "Jesus Christ, Joy Parker." She calls me by my full name, as if she were my mother or something. Though my mother never says my whole name, annoyed or not; I guess because the "Parker" reminds her of my father or something. She just says "Jesus Christ, Joy." Jesus Christ is not really part of my name, but it seems to go with "Joy." Like a Christmas card.

When we finally got to the edge of the world, it was kind of disappointing. There were too many trees for one thing, dishonestly green, as if I wouldn't remember that a few months ago they had probably been dead wood, just like the ones on Utopia Parkway. Across the street was what Marisa insisted on calling the beach, though it looked like a sinkhole. The sand seemed like dirt, more brown than the silvery white I liked. The waves weren't big enough to even ruffle my ankles, not that I was going to step in the water anyway. It wasn't just that it wasn't blue. It had garbage in it. Plastic bags and crack vials and syringes.

"Medical waste," Marisa said.

I nodded. But she couldn't fool me. It was junkie debris. The trash of people so sad that they needed a fix before they could appreciate a walk on the beach. Though I had to admit, seeing the world looking this scummy made me want to get so high that I could look down and it wouldn't matter.

"It's beautiful, isn't it?" Marisa asked as she put her cigarette out in the dirt/sand.

I nodded, afraid I was going to cry.

But then she kissed me so soft and so hard all at once, it was almost as if I could hear the ocean. It was almost as if the ocean were kissing me, instead of Marisa. Or maybe with Marisa. Both of them kissing me and me kissing both of them.

Sometimes I kiss the floor, pretending it is the ocean and Marisa. Pretending it is that too-cold spring day when we cut school and rode the subway far from Utopia Parkway to Rockaway Beach. Pretending the damn attendance officer never called my mother. I let my tongue slip from between my lips, licking the blue linoleum. It tastes a little like a cigarette, like Marisa and the ocean.

But the floor never kisses me back.

*T*he kitchen floor is an eye. The captive blue of the linoleum as dull as the wolf eye. The other eye is brown; I can see that although the animal has its head tilted away from the television camera. A beautiful sweet brown, like the best chocolate, like Marisa's eyes. But the eye the TV focused on is blue, veined with icicles of white. It makes the animal look ferocious, just like it is supposed to.

Although I thought wolf eyes were yellow. Or maybe that's just true in spooky movies. I could ask someone, but there is no one here to ask. The days seem so long. So, I just say it out loud, testing its truth. "Yellow," I say. The color of piss, I don't say, because then I might remember that I have to pee and I haven't peed all day because if I pee in the bucket I will have to look at it, and its yellow embarrasses me.

So I look at the television set, pretending it is a window. The wolf sits on the other side of the window behind another window, this one of wire. The wire window is on a truck, lettered in red: ANIMAL CONTROL. The wolf looks depressed.

The reporter is gorgeous. I like this one. She has a smooth Spanish accent, lulling and friendly, even when she tries to sound strict. Like now. As she tells us, her faithful viewers, about this dangerous animal. A wolf. Being kept as a pet. Her voice lilts: "Just off Utopia Parkway, in the greenery of Queens." A wolf, found in the yard, chained to a clothesline pole. The neighbors complained at the howling. Animal Control was called. They came with their truck, lettered in red.

"Chained all day," the reporter says, as if she feels sorry for the animal. She reminds me of Marisa. So serious and soft. Although Marisa would probably crack some comment about how pathetic the wolf looked. Not like anything wild and dangerous. Not like something that killed grizzly bears in the wilderness. More like a German shepherd with mange.

"Mange—that's what happens when you live in Queens," I would say to Marisa. Or maybe I wouldn't. After all, Marisa lives in Queens.

I wonder where Marisa is. I heard her in the alley the other night. It was dark, so it must have been late, and her voice funneled up between the car alarms and radios. I heard her clear as day. Heard her ask for me. Heard my mother tell her I had gone back to Florida; heard Marisa say she didn't believe my mother; heard my mother call Marisa a "lesbo-slut."

I wonder if the man on the television set, the one hiding his who-knows-what-color-eyes behind sunglasses, is sorry about chaining the wolf. I wonder if he will go to jail or what will happen to him. I wonder whether he is still wearing sunglasses.

I wonder what will happen to the wolf.

I wonder if that is my mother coming up the stairs with Chinese food for me. I hope she brought sweet and sour. I love sweet and sour. But it sounds like too many voices to be my mother. Too many voices outside the door, one of them knocking, one of them barking out "Joy Parker," all of them past the uncrossable blue ocean of linoleum.

PART TWO: WOMEN

Kia Townsend always wanted to be a photographer, but her business card labels her a juvenile attorney. The card was supposed to read, "Juvenile Rights Attorney," making it clear that it is not she who is a juvenile, but only the people she represents. When she complained to her boss, he told her the government printers were probably trying to save ink because of the budget crisis. Although he winked in a way that made her think that the omission was probably ideological: The government was not keen on rights, whether for juveniles or anyone else. When Kia was feeling most jaded, like today, she knew that the omission was not budgetary or political: It was simply incompetence.

If she were a photographer, she knew she would choose to work only in black and white. Those were her family colors. Black on the paternal; white on the maternal. Making her a thousand shades of gray. Never white enough; never black enough. Everyone in Queens always assumes she is Puerto Rican, her beautiful brown tan turned ashen by the ridiculous winters. Sometimes people thought she was being rude when they started to speak Spanish to her and she shrugged her shoulders. Although it was better to be her gray/brown self here than in some places; at least that's what she told herself, and it usually seemed true when she remembered the places she had been.

Though in her office near Utopia Parkway, it could be hard to believe that any place else on earth was worse. The air-conditioning is not working and the reception room of the Law Guardian Unit of Legal Aid is clogged with the screaming kids and sullen adolescents who are the clients. And dotted with hostile parents; even the nicest parents ultimately become hostile. It was difficult for them to understand why their children had to have attorneys, paid for by the state, no less.

Kia has three memorandums of law due by Friday. But it's difficult to write because she is emergency attorney of the day. Every case seems to be an emergency, especially on this humid June afternoon.

She looks at the newest petition for neglect and abuse, a hearing scheduled immediately for a kid who had been removed less than an hour ago. IN RE: JOY PARKER, A CHILD UNDER THE AGE OF EIGHTEEN YEARS OF AGE. The charging paragraph alleged that the fifteen-year-old had been chained to a radiator by her mother for the last several weeks, having to use a bucket to go to the bathroom, and having only a television set for company.

Jesus Christ, Kia says out loud.

As she puts the petition in her briefcase, she wishes she were not a juvenile attorney, forget whether or not rights were involved. She wishes she had become a photographer instead of taking one as a lover. Kia wishes her lover were here right now, so that Kia could kiss her lover's neck and tell her lover how wonderful she is.

Kia's wonderful lover is screaming at another woman. At the moment that Kia is walking over to the courtroom, the fresh file folder containing the petition for neglect and abuse of the minor child Joy Parker jutting from her overstuffed briefcase, Summer is standing on the public side of a bulletproof-glass window yelling at the receptionist of the North Shore Animal Shelter.

Almost any receptionist would keep Summer on the outside of the glass. Summer's screams make the hundreds of chains around her neck seem to vibrate and the stained front of her dress pull tighter across her chest. There's some design on her cheek that looks as if it was drawn with cheap eyeliner, although it could be an artless tattoo. She has some piercings, filled mostly with silver rings, around her eyebrows, through her nostril, on her lip.

And Summer's hair is matted and braided with feathers and scraps of fur collected from the floor of one wilderness or another. She has plenty of opportunities to steal or purchase plumes or skins to decorate herself with exotic indulgence, but she thinks it is unthinkable to endanger the wildlife she captures with her high-powered zoom. For, in addition to being a photographer, Summer is an animal rights activist. So she is relegated the discards, although she prefers to think of them as gifts.

Just the way Summer thinks of Kia: as a gift. She tries to treat Kia as if Kia is the rarest of creatures, the most profound of pets, yet also as an absolute peer. If it were not for this unwavering equality, Kia—wary of being exoticized—would have abandoned Summer long ago. Would have left her, in fact, where she found her: in a bathtub in South Carolina.

Kia, thinking she was going north from Florida, had traveled deeper south when she went to college at the University of South Carolina. She had imagined hills, rolling green, pastoral enough to make her a poet if not a photographer. She had not imagined that people would ask her whether she was white or black, that one of the people who would ask her was a famous writer and English professor who smelled of whiskey and pawed at her breasts while they were the only two people stranded in an elevator between the sixth and seventh floors of the liberal arts building; that the only place people did not question her color was at what seemed to be the only interracial bar in town, which was also the gay bar.

Soon, Kia was spending more time at the bar than in the liberal arts building or in the dorm room she shared with a white girl from Aiken who called her "my colored roomie." Explaining that to the black woman at the residence office made it easier to get her housing deposit back. To her mother, Kia wrote that escaping the dorms would make it easier to study, although she knew her mother would tell her that Kia shouldn't be deciding she hated dorm life after only six weeks. As soon as she posted the letter, she embarked on a search for off-campus housing, collecting phone numbers off bulletin boards and visiting homes that needed another person. Which was how she first saw Summer in the bathtub.

The house was brick and in the country on a few acres that Kia guessed had once been sharecropped. Kia had misgivings about her car's reliability as well as the number of roommates and rules. Over the phone, a woman named Arlene spewed words like *collective* and *vegetarianism* and *racial harmony* and *consciousness*. But when Kia saw the place, she was thrilled: She would have her own bedroom, the living room was large, the kitchen larger, and there was even a fireplace. Plenty of space and cheap as dirt. Perhaps she could set up a darkroom. Perhaps she could write poetry. Perhaps it would become obvious to her what her major should be. Maybe political science or something far from the liberal arts building.

And the house smelled good. Not like food, or like the flowers that still bloomed outside, but like something ethereal and expensive. Finally she asked.

"Oh, that's just VitaBath," her guide Arlene laughed. "Miss Chocolate is doing her bubble routine. You'll get used to it."

Kia smiled at the prediction. It must mean that she was passing the housemate test. Although she wondered whether she'd ever get used to the way white people talked in this state. Really, *Miss Chocolate*? As if it weren't bad enough, Arlene had mentioned the black member of the collective at least three times, as if that were some sort of credential. If she moved in, what would they be calling her? Miss White Chocolate?

"You really should meet her anyway," Arlene said, motioning Kia to follow down the hall. The bathroom door was open, the smell becoming too pungent to remain pleasant. Before Kia could decide whether or not she was being rude, she was standing on a plush purple rug in the middle of the bathroom and the woman in the bathtub was standing up, extending her hand, introducing herself as Summer.

Kia fumbled. Not just because Summer was naked, except for a silver necklace with some sort of round charm and the residuals of bubbles, which clung to her body. There was a way in which Summer was naked, as an affront almost, a challenge. There was nothing sexual about it; it was antisexual. It was provocative only in the sense that any viewer felt as if she was being provoked to find Summer remotely seductive. It was a stance that Kia would come to know well. But it wasn't the expanse of skin that most startled Kia, it was its shade. Pale, even though reddened from the hot water. Pale enough so that Kia could see the woman's veins like little rivers in the landscape of her thighs.

The night of the day Kia moved in, Arlene and Summer and Janice sat by the fireplace, all of them smoking dope and feeling friendly. Kia recognized Janice from the bar, a tall black woman with a very short 'fro. Arlene kept glancing at

Janice, as if waiting for applause for having located Kia. Summer was naked, except for an afghan, which covered the rivers in her thighs.

"Don't hog the reefer, Miss Chocolate," Arlene said, laughing.

"Fuck you," Summer said, handing over the joint.

"Why does everyone call you Miss Chocolate?" Kia blurted, the marijuana blurring her Southern manners.

"I'm allergic." Summer smiled.

"Tell the fucking truth." Arlene laughed.

"I am."

"She's an heiress," Janice announced, "to a chocolate fortune."

"Not without a fight. I'm thinking of suing."

"Did they cut you out of a will?" Kia risked, still not knowing how much was polite.

"No one's dead. It's more complicated than that." Summer's voice was soft and blended with the noises from the fire.

"You might as well tell her," Arlene said softly. "Before she hears it from someone else."

"I might sue my father. My mother was the household maid he raped; that's how I was born. And then he started raping me when I was fourteen."

"I didn't know white maids got raped." Kia covered her mouth, but it was too late.

Summer laughed. "They do. Happens to all kinds of people, from what I hear these days. Men will rape anything; color doesn't matter." Summer laughed again. "But I'm lucky enough that my rapist is rich as shit. At least that's what my lawyer says."

Summer tried to blow a smoke ring, but the dope only curled in a desultory spiral.

Later, Kia would learn all the details: the abortion, the attempted suicide of the chocolate baron's legitimate daughter, the anger of Summer's own mother, who thought Summer should be quiet and maybe the old man would send her to college. Later, Kia would realize this was the precise moment her

life changed: She decided to go to law school. Later, after Kia
fell in love with Summer.

Summer, screaming Summer. Screaming at the receptionist
at the North Shore Animal Shelter, where the animal everyone
was calling a wolf had been taken by Animal Control.

*F*rom their usual table, Summer and Kia fill the emptiness of Lorenzo's Restaurant with sounds. Mrs. Lorenzo, who did not change her name or her job despite her divorce, dotes on her only customers, refills their water glasses every time either of them takes a sip. Mr. Lorenzo, who reflexively attempts to inspire jealousy, smiles too broadly as he brings Summer's year-round drink, "Coke, no ice," and Kia's summer glass of iced coffee. Even before the effects of the caffeine, however, the women's conversation accelerates.

If how they talk could properly be called a conversation.

This evening, they conform to a pattern fashioned over hundreds of dinners at the end of difficult days, many of the recent ones occurring at Lorenzo's Restaurant, not far from their apartment in Queens, on the other side of Utopia Parkway. An arrangement of voices that began in a farmhouse in South Carolina, Summer most often in her tub of VitaBath and Kia sitting on the purple plush of the rug. Continuing while Summer's lawyer negotiated a piece of the chocolate fortune and Kia fussed with her personal essays for law school applications. Not decreasing even when Summer and Kia moved to New York, and other people swirled around them, people who were photographers or animal activists like Summer or law students and then lawyers like Kia, people who prided themselves on manners or empathy or both, people who could have a proper conversation over cocktails.

But Kia and Summer never pretend they are having a conversation over cocktails, even cocktails of Coke and coffee. It is more like switching channels during the monologues of those two guys who are still competing to be Johnny Carson, at least according to Mrs. Lorenzo. It is more like a pair of parallel lines, a Morse code broken by pauses of listening, at least according to Mr. Lorenzo. Like two teenagers smoking two cigarettes. Like the tracks left by some sleek animal on the unforgiving floor of the tundra.

"And then, the asshole Animal Control guy calls me a girl and talks to me like I'm some fucking fifteen-year-old and tells me the wolf is a dangerous, wild creature that belongs in a cage. If motherfuckers like him hadn't decimated the wilderness so they could wipe their asses with Charmin and eat off goddamn paper plates . . ."

"So, the social workers went to the apartment on a tip. I think one of the child's friends called them. I'm not sure whether they knocked the door down. They always fudge that part. Found her handcuffed to the kitchen radiator. Her ankle."

"Probably not a wolf anyway because there are hybrids all over the goddamn country. But it's some sort of New York law—you'll need to look this up for me, Kia, if you can—that it's the same thing anyway. If the animal is wolf at all, even a tiny percent wolf and ninety percent dog, it can be treated like a wolf. Which isn't good because it means that the asshole owner probably didn't have a fucking federal permit to keep a wolf and the animal can be taken away for it's own fucking protection, and we all know what that means."

"She's from Florida. Moved here with her mother and her mother's boyfriend. Wouldn't say too much at first. Asked me if I could call her friend for her. But then changed her mind. Started to cry. Said the friend was why she got in trouble with her mother."

"It's got to be a wolf-dog. I mean, with a blue eye like that, it's no wolf. Pups, yes, they'll have blue eyes, but this animal is no pup. You know how the fuck it happens, don't you? People breed these animals because they think they can have wilderness and man's best friend rolled into one. Remember that woman we knew in South Carolina that had the owl that kept dropping mice on her while she was sleeping? Well, when it doesn't work out, when the wild animal acts like a wild animal, shitting in the house or making noises that would raise the dead, then the people can't understand why the fuck it's happening."

"I'm going to have a hard time with this one, Summer. My job is to represent Joy. That's the child. Not a child, fifteen. Which means she's too old for me to substitute judgment. To say what I think is best for her instead of what she wants. But she might want to go back, especially after she's stayed in the shelter a few days."

"People think they're damn vampires or something. I mean, they've been hunted throughout history and had bounties on them, can you fucking believe it? Exterminated from Europe by a bunch of hysterical men and the ranchers in the United States haven't been much better, probably even more hysterical. And the reason? Get this, the reason for all this hatred is that wolves kill to eat, like humans don't, like these ranchers raising cattle are all the world's biggest vegetarian advocates."

"It's not just the radiator. Or the handcuffs. Or the bucket for a bathroom. She thinks her mother locked her up because she cut school and kissed her girlfriend. That's what she implied. I'll have to talk to the mother. Want to talk to her before she testifies. But she wasn't in court."

"Though maybe the owner can prove it's a dog—one hundred percent dog—at least then there wouldn't be such panic. I mean, they had news crews out there from television stations, like there aren't a hundred horrible things happening in Queens, not to mention the rest of the city. What, nothing else is happening except that we have a barking dog complaint?"

"Placed Joy in the shelter. She seemed scared. She's not street-smart. Could hardly look at me. I don't want to think about what she's doing right now. She's not going to have an easy time of it tonight. I need to get over there in the morning. And talk to her mother tomorrow."

"Then that bitch at the North Shore Animal Shelter. I'm

telling you, I'm going to have her head on a plate, her teased hair ripped out, and her excuse for a brain looking like refried beans. I should call Fox—you remember my friend Fox—I think her father's on the board of the shelter and she dates the director or maybe she's dating the vet in charge, I forget which. This shelter is supposed to be the best one, the most humane— humane, isn't that a joke?—the most humane one around here, but people only think that because it's on fucking Long Island. I am definitely going to get in touch with Fox about this, first thing in the morning, even if I wake the bitch up."

"This system makes me sick sometimes. I mean, it's the mother who should be locked up. Not Joy."

"I can't believe what might happen to such a beautiful animal."

Mr. and Mrs. Lorenzo would not believe that both Kia and Summer had each heard every word her lover had uttered, perhaps because neither Mr. nor Mrs. Lorenzo ever heard the quieter comments. Or followed Kia and Summer out to their van, a ten-year-old Dodge Caravan in suburban navy blue, but airbrushed with a giant fluorescent dolphin arcing from whitecaps as if it were a Volkswagen bus and it were 1968 instead of thirty years later.

They are in the van only a few seconds when Summer removes her hand from the gearshift and puts it on Kia's knee.

"All that, just because she might be a dyke? Jesus fucking Christ."

Kia shakes her head in reply.

"You're a wonderful woman, you know that, my Kia? You're really doing wonderful work. You're going to make sure that kid gets what she wants. Not what the stupid social workers want. And not what her crazy homophobe of a mother wants, and not only are you great, you're fucking cute!"

Kia smiles. "You aren't so bad yourself. But really, all that commotion just because it might be a wolf?"

And that night, in their bed in their apartment, Summer's hands in Kia's curls, Kia's fingers snagging in Summer's weavings of feather and fur, they kiss as if there is no tomorrow.

Summer has the key. A ring of keys, actually, because more than one key has become necessary to achieve almost anything. And Summer wants to achieve something. Something grand and treacherous. Something stupendous. Yet simple.

Simple if Summer could figure out which key was appropriate where. If Fox were here, Fox could help. And Fox should be here, Summer growls. Fox, her friend—or perhaps former friend—who used to be so radical about animal rights. Radical enough to rename herself and write a dissertation about the arctic fox. But now, when something can be done that isn't just writing a letter to a congressperson or buying an endangered species calendar or doing yet another study with a volcano of footnotes, Fox has gotten timid. Summer had sought assistance from Fox but Fox had replied with platitudes about limits and risks, about her future as an academic.

But, Summer had noticed, Fox had mostly talked about her new girlfriend, the Chief Veterinarian. How Fox could not betray her. How Fox could not disappoint her. How Fox thought she loved her, thought she really loved her. And Summer had thought, but had not said, how can you love a woman, really or otherwise, who is the chief veterinarian for an animal shelter? Don't you know what that means? She's the supervisor of extermination. She's a murderer. No, Summer had not said that to Fox. Because she didn't need to. She knew that Fox was already thinking that. She could feel Fox feeling it. Feeling the deaths.

It had been something Fox had had to overcome before she even went to the movies with the Chief Veterinarian. They had seen a popular disaster movie, and Summer had heard about the exact moment the Chief Veterinarian had put her hand so casually on Fox's knee. By the time, several movies and progressively more lingering touches later, they had fallen into bed at Fox's apartment, Fox seemed completely accepting of the Chief Veterinarian's role at the animal shelter.

Although maybe Fox hadn't gotten over it, not completely. Because Fox had given Summer the ring of keys. The ring of keys that the Chief Veterinarian had lost. The ring of keys that Fox had found burrowed among the dust bunnies under her bed, weeks after the Chief Veterinarian had given up hope and had replaced them. The ring of keys that Fox had simply placed on the counter between herself and Summer, not handing them to Summer, but not stopping her from picking them up. The ring of keys that Summer is holding in her hands right now. Holding in her hands, outside the animal shelter, after it has closed, while the summer sun still flares.

The last commuters, with their desperate strides, have long since passed by the back of the animal shelter, taking a shortcut from the train station to their homes, through the alley where Summer's van is now parked. No one lingers on the short street, the dead-end street, the barely paved lane in front of the animal shelter. The many who dropped off unwanted animals today and the few who came to adopt are dispersed through the suburbs. The workers too have gone home to their summer suppers of chicken and coleslaw, including the receptionist whom Summer had screamed at the last time she had been here.

There seems to be no one to spy on Summer, a woman who, if anyone had been spying, might have been judged as slightly dangerous, or at the very least someone who did not belong on Long Island. Most alarming was Summer's head of tangled feathers and tiny braids woven with pieces of fur, her patch of skull shaved as if from some surgical procedure. Her dress was not any more reassuring; it was the dress of an old woman or an overgrown doll, gingham: key-lime-green checks offset by squares of dirty white meringue. The hem had been made by pinking sheers.

The smallest key on the ring confirms Summer's belief that there will be an alarm. After she gets inside, through the thick metal door, all she has to do is locate the alarm and figure out how to shut it off. And if she doesn't? Only a few minutes to escape. Her fingers caress the smallest key. Yes, the small key means it is not a combination, some secret series of numbers that she would never be able to guess in a million years. Nevertheless, she is sweating in the cool evening. A trickle runs down her back, blotted by the green and white gingham.

She thinks for a moment that she could simply walk through the concrete wall. Forget the ring of keys. Forget the steel door and the locks and the alarm. But that is not the way things are done. She listens for something that might tell her otherwise. There is only silence until she hears a train.

Once inside, she cannot hear the train. And she can no longer hear the silence. All she can hear is the screaming.

Terrible screaming. Not out-loud screaming, but screaming that comes from the inside. Inside her own flesh. From inside the marrow of her bones, that delicious part of her that could be sucked out if she were a meal. Screaming so intense that she almost forgets about the alarm, until the smallest key presses itself into her palm and then seduces the little red box. The alarm so innocent, so brilliantly obvious, so metallically quiet in the midst of the din.

She is in hell. Hell will be loud, Summer knows.

And hell will not be filled with fire, but with wire. There are wires everywhere. Cages behind cages. Neat in rows on the other side of a wall of wire. There is a wire door in the wire wall. It has a lock, but the lock is not wire. The keys, though, feel sharp as wires in Summer's hand. She tries one and then another until she finds the one that slips into the lock as precisely as Fox's tongue must have slipped into the Chief Veterinarian on the afternoon she lost her keys.

Don't think about that, a voice says. Not Summer's voice,

but inside Summer. Somewhere different from the place where the screaming originates. But close, close to that soft marrow.

Summer presses her back teeth together and begins to move among the cages.

She had expected the dogs. And the cats. But there are more raccoons than she thought there would be. And a few skunks; she hadn't really considered skunks. And a rabbit as large as an armadillo. Summer loves armadillos. The range of their voices. She doesn't hear any armadillos in this shelter.

She is searching for a large cage, the goal of her breaking and entering. She is looking for the wolf. The wolf with the one blue eye. The wolf-dog, a hybrid of some sort. Taken from Queens, driven on Utopia Parkway to this shelter on Long Island because the city shelters prefer not to accommodate "wild animals." Taken from the man who had kept the wolf chained in the small yard. The man is being charged with animal cruelty. The wolf-dog is being scheduled for destruction.

Summer is here to rescue the wolf, the wolf-dog, before it is killed.

Before it is put down, as the Chief Veterinarian might say. If she were saying at all. Even when Summer telephoned, pretending to be from a newspaper, the receptionist had replied with an officious "We are not at liberty to release any information." But Summer knew. Summer knew.

And Kia, Summer's lover, had confirmed it. It had not taken Kia the lawyer very long to find the New York statute that provided that any part-wolf, part-dog animal was to be considered a wolf. And treated as such. A wolf and therefore a wild animal and therefore not able to be possessed by any ordinary person. A person would need a special permit and the Department of Wildlife was not granting those permits to "ordinary citizens." "What does that mean?" Summer had asked. "You have to be a dealer in exotic animals," Kia replied. Summer had predictably exploded into a tirade about commerce and exploitation and profit while Kia almost listened.

It had not taken Kia that much longer to locate the regulations and policies of animal shelters dealing with unadoptable wild animals. There was even a new regulation prohibiting the sale of the wild animal to laboratories because it was not humane. "Humane!" Summer had squealed when she had heard that word. Unlike Kia, Summer's research was not done with books, or even on computers. Summer got into her van and drove around Queens, crossing Utopia Parkway now and then, thinking about that artist who had lived on this street with his mother and brother for thirty-some years. The one who made little boxes, collages of disconnected images that somehow made sense, miniature worlds bounded by wood and glass.

Then she came back home and settled into a beige chair with pink roses, rescued from some refuse pile on bulk collection day. She started to dial the phone and to put numbers and names on one of Kia's yellow legal pads until she was satisfied.

"Havre de Loup," Summer announced to Kia.

Kia's language skills, mostly derived from the high school Latin so beneficial during law school, were sufficiently competent to piece together the idea of a wolf sanctuary.

"Where is it?"

"Quebec."

"So that explains the French," Kia said, "but how will they get the wolf-dog? Is there some sort of program or something?"

"We are the program," Summer said. She looked at Kia for a long time and Kia looked back, neither one of them twitching. Their love stretched between them, flat and heavy and taut. Kia finally closed her eyes.

"Let me decide on my own, Summer," Kia said.

"I am." Summer smiled. For she knew then that Kia would, that Kia was only making sure that she wasn't being overpowered by Summer's desires, that Kia was only testing the voice inside her head to make sure it was her own.

Kia turned away from Summer and suggested they go to dinner. To Lorenzo's, their usual restaurant. It wasn't until the door to Lorenzo's was closing behind them and Summer was driving them home in the van that Kia had said: "OK. But it will have to be the weekend. I'll get Monday off or something. And remember, I have to work a little late on Friday. I need to observe a visit at the park, between the girl Joy and her mother."

Summer hurries now, thinking of Kia, who will be waiting when Summer casually pulls up, the girl in the park having visited with the mother who had abused her, the wolf safely in the carrier in the back of the van. Oh damn, the carrier! She left it in the van. Well, she'll simply walk the wolf back to the alley on a leash—a rope or something—like an ordinary dog. If she can even find the damn animal. Too many cages. All this wire is giving her a headache. Which makes it difficult to hear. To hear the wolf's voice among all the other screams.

Summer walks back toward the door, toward the alarm. From this far wall, she retrieves the largest-size collar and leash on the display. Rips the small tag from the imitation leather. Overpriced, Summer notes. A small exploitation of the people who come to adopt the animals that would otherwise be exterminated. "You'll need a collar and leash," Summer can almost hear the receptionist saying, her voice liltingly sweet. "Oh, yes," the new owner will reply. And shell out some money.

Then she scans the concrete hell. Listening. Listening.

Suddenly startled by an absence more ugly than the incessant screaming. She walks toward the pool of silence. Past and through the labyrinth of metal mesh. Finally sees the mute animal in the cage and certainly it has one blue, unblinking eye. But it doesn't look like a noble wolf. Or even a mangy coyote. It looks excessively average, like a dog. Pitiful. But then, what doesn't look pitiful dissected by wires?

Summer bends her head close. Listening. Hoping to hear, what? Not the horrible screaming that is coming from inside the other animals, but something else. Some majestic sound that will convince her that her risk is a worthwhile one. Some voice. Sensate and sensible.

The wolf-dog maintains its silence.

Summer shifts from foot to foot, waiting for some sign,

smelling the harsh metal. That same metal smell when the man who was her father came to her fourteen-year-old body. He must have always shaved first, some flecks of his steel razor remaining on the face he pressed into her. Or maybe the metal was from the huge candy machines he kissed in order to make his fortune. His breathing was noisy, noisier than any factory, roaring in her ears. This was when she learned to hear voices, to hear screams. To be so still and silent that what was deep inside could wrap itself around language and vibrate into voices.

This was when she tried to bend back the cage of his body with her fingers until they bled. Too many nights they bled. And she tried to tell her mother about the blood running down her hands, but her mother probably couldn't hear her over the screaming. Or perhaps it was too noisy to hear anything, even your daughter, when you were cleaning toilets in the home of the man. In the home of the man's wife. They were always having a party. The man and his wife. And sometimes Summer's mother, one of the maids, brought leftovers back to the little cottage.

The metal tells her to relax. To forget. It sings the lullaby of denial. The suck of giving up. How easy to slip through the thin silvery wires. To curl next to the wolf-dog. To wait until it is the correct time to die.

The wolf-dog's fur is softer than Summer thought it would be. Too much dog and not enough wolf. A wolf would have wire for hair. A wolf would have not been caught like this. A real wolf would be ferocious and have two yellow eyes that could burn a hole through the hell of the wires. A real girl would not let her father rape her.

Summer puts her nose next to the wolf-dog's nose. Summer inhales the animal's exhale. Summer sniffs the dampness from its nostrils. Summer puts one hand on each of the animal's ears, as if she is going to pull it even closer and kiss it deeply. But she doesn't. Doesn't pull it closer and doesn't kiss it. Doesn't have to. There is no need. There is nothing more.

She is in the cage with the wolf-dog because this is all she deserves. Or she deserves worse, really. Yes, much worse.

The man who was her father—although she didn't know he was her father then, didn't know until much later, when her mother told her—had kissed her neck, once. A little farewell peck. Nothing vampirish about it.

Nothing wet or selfish. Just a simple kiss. On the neck.

And it was nice.

So nice that Summer had started to sob. She had not cried before, not while he was still there anyway. She had not cried when she bled from trying to bend back the steel smell from his body. She had not cried when he had put his knee between her legs and forced open the branches of her body. She had not cried when his heaviness collapsed on her chest, so that she felt as if she would suffocate although she was still breathing. No, she hadn't cried. Until now.

And he hugged her then.

And she hugged him back.

She hugged him back.

She could hug the wolf-dog now. She was so close she could twine herself with the unexpected softness, kiss the wolf's moist black nose, cry in the wolf's muscular neck. She belongs with the animal. Belongs in the cage, waiting to be exterminated. Waiting for the receptionist, the Chief Veterinarian, the assistant who will administer the lethal injection.

Don't be a dry stream.

The voice is in her head.

The voice must belong to the wolf-dog. Yes, it is so rough and impatient. So wolf. It is a few octaves lower than the screams, but still a few octaves higher than she would have imagined. If she had imagined. Which she hadn't, not really. Not clearly enough.

Hadn't imagined being here. What would come next. Hadn't thought it through. "We need to think things through," her lawyer had said. A feminist lawyer, a good woman, a woman who took time with her, acting almost as a therapist instead of a lawyer. The feminist lawyer who had taken her case. Had sued the man who was her father, the man who sexually abused her, the man with a lot of money who should give her some. And he did. He did. The feminist lawyer settled the case for a comfortable sum. A sum that made everyone feel comfortable. A sum that was supposed to help Summer feel as if she wasn't still in the cage of him.

She was supposed to be the alpha wolf. Yes, that's what she had imagined. Was supposed to be a leader. In control. Inspire confidence. Be someone to follow. And then lead them both out of here.

She wasn't supposed to be in a cage.

Not anymore.

Never.

Summer feels the keys in her hand. Sharp keys. Heavy keys. But none of them call out to her to fit the lock of the cage. Because there is no lock. Just a latch. A simple latch.

Summer snorts.

The wolf-dog remains sullen, biting at a paw that does not have fingers, a paw that can tear and scratch but not unlatch.

Summer opens the door of the cage.

The wolf-dog does not lunge. Summer flattens her palm toward the wolf-dog. Commands, "Come." The wolf-dog doesn't move.

They repeat their dance.

Flat palm.

"Come."

Motionlessness.

Summer reaches into the cage. Bares her own teeth. Pulls the wolf-dog by the scruff of the neck. Slips the collar over its head. Tugs on the attached leash.

No.

The wolf-dog's voice is less impatient than before, more determined.

"Listen," Summer says in her best alpha-wolf voice, "we are leaving this place before you get killed. You don't want to have a short life spent in a goddamn cage, do you?"

Others.

"Oh, this is a fine fucking time for charity. We can't perform the rescue of the century."

Though now, once she has heard the voice over the screams, had the idea in the spaces between the screams, she knows she cannot free only the wolf-dog.

And besides, this will be more sensible. It won't point so directly toward a search for the wolf-dog. It will seem more accidental. Inexplicable. All the animals escaped. Found a set of keys under the bed and the racoons opened all the locks. Or maybe a fire? Can one set hell on fire? All this steel and concrete? Even if . . . no, too dangerous.

But it is not the wolf-dog's voice inside Summer's head giving reasons and rationalizations. Giving a concrete shape to the plan: The rabbit first or last? The skunks and raccoons? Cats, then dogs? It is Summer's voice. Only Summer.

Only Summer, admiring the lope of the wolf-dog as she guides it out the door, down the lane, back to the alley, into the van. What once were screams inside Summer are now howls and yelps, outside the world of the wires. Summer is surrounded by the sounds of trapped animals enjoying their escape, even if it proves temporary.

Maybe all escapes are temporary.

Maybe not.

Summer asks the wolf-dog what it thinks as she navigates the van on the crowded highway, toward the waiting Kia and the girl Joy.

It doesn't answer.

"Don't be a dry stream," Summer says, smiling.

She wonders how a wolf-dog smiles. If she could twist around and see inside the carrier, could she tell if the animal was smiling? Or is the carrier too much like a cage for the wolf-dog to smile? How can she tell it about the plan to transport it to Quebec? To a place where it can run free, among wolves and hybrids. How can she convince it she means no harm?

Keys.

Summer hears the command, the question, the slightly less sullen voice inside herself and wants to laugh. Thinking of the Chief Veterinarian and the man who was her father, Summer realizes that she—maybe more than the killer or the rapist—is the criminal, with an animal for an accomplice and a possible plea of insanity and a piece of evidence. She wipes the keys off on her gingham dress and throws them out the window, into the summer twilight, contributing to the garbage that lines the Utopia Parkway.

Among the other people in Flushing Meadows Corona Park this Friday evening, Kia is sitting on a bench, watching Joy Parker and Joy's mother, Loretta. The daughter and mother are sitting on another park bench, closer to the giant silver globe surrounded by fountains. The daughter and mother with the same slight frames, the same tilt of the head on the neck, the same odd wrap of one ankle around the other. They do not touch. They do not talk. The daughter and mother do not know what to do, what to say, and the fact that Kia is watching them does not give them any clues.

Joy Parker's social worker, the woman who brought Joy to the park to visit her mother, has gone off somewhere to do something. To buy a Coke or a cup of coffee. To make a phone call. To have a cigarette. Kia does not remember what the social worker said, but thinks she should be back by now. The long summer twilight is starting, the sky twinged with lavender above the thin trees.

The social worker and her boyfriend admire the sky when they are not kissing in the front seat of his car, parked in the lot behind the Queens Museum, an unimpressive building facing the fountain-ringed silver globe.

Kia cannot see the lot with the red parked car that belongs to the social worker's boyfriend. Kia can see that Loretta has started crying. She can't see the tears or the reddening nose, but there is some change in position, some slight conflation of face and hand. Kia can see the grief, the regret, but also something else. A glitter that makes Joy stiffen. And stand up. Walk toward Kia.

"Where's Ms. Swedlowe?"

"Your social worker? I don't know. Said she'd be right back."

"Well, the visit's over. I'm ready to go."

"Something wrong?"

"No. But this is too hard. She's crying. And I'm not going to feel sorry for her."

Kia doesn't answer. She just waves at Loretta's back as Loretta walks around the fountains until she is out of sight, obscured by the spray. Kia half expects her to appear on the other side of the globe, circling back. But Loretta does not appear.

So Kia waits with Joy for the social worker.

Kia is also looking for Summer, who should be here any time now. If all has gone well. If she hasn't been caught breaking and . . . doing whatever it is she is doing. Kia didn't want to know. Kia was, after all, as she reminded herself, an attorney. A juvenile *rights* attorney. Representing juveniles who have run afoul of the law. Kids who have been accused of breaking and entering, although usually not animal shelters to rescue a wolf. And kids who have done nothing wrong at all, except to be born to the wrong parents, parents who would take a belt to a kid's bare flesh because they have had a bad day, or a mother, like Joy's mother, who would chain her only daughter to a radiator to prevent her from becoming a dyke.

And then gets a dyke as an attorney.

I should run through the fountains and catch Loretta, tell her that her daughter now has a dyke for an attorney, Kia thinks. That would shock her. Or maybe it wouldn't. Maybe she would just think that's more proof of the global threat of lesbianism.

Kia doesn't want to think about the trial. How uncomfortable it is going to be. How the judge will look over his glasses at Kia when the word *lesbian* is used. If it gets that far.

Can't we settle this? Kia can hear herself saying, out in the hallway, the morning of the scheduled trial.

But before she gets that far, she'll have to figure out what her client, Joy Parker—fifteen-year-old Joy Parker—wants. Now, Kia knows, is not a good time to ask her. It is never a good time to ask about ultimate plans after one of her kids—one of her clients—has seen a parent. It is absolutely the worst time.

So Kia tries to make conversation. Idle conversation.

Kia thinks about asking Joy to name the seven continents that protrude from the skeleton of silver that is the globe.

No, that sounds like a test.

Perhaps ask her what continent is her favorite.

But that also sounds like a test, albeit more subjective. Kia knows she wouldn't be satisfied with a simple answer: Asia, Australia, Africa. She'd press the girl to make an argument, supporting her choice.

Or maybe she could ask her something about those silver rings around the globe. Three of them. Orbits or something, she supposes. Maybe that would be something to discuss with this adolescent.

She's still undecided when she spots Summer's van coming toward them on the NO UNAUTHORIZED VEHICLES road.

Kia realizes how much she does not want this to happen. Does not want Summer to come to pick her up so that they can drive all night to Quebec before Joy Parker has been escorted back to the foster home by her social worker. Does not want Joy Parker to see Summer. Or the van. Or the wolf-dog.

But Summer is out of the van before Kia can think of a delaying tactic.

"Cool van," Joy says, although she is looking at Summer's tangled and bedecked hair, Summer's green-checked gingham dress with the zigzag hem, Summer's loose collar of strands of silver necklaces, Summer's wild expression.

"Summer, Joy. Joy, Summer." Kia's introduction is formal, businesslike, lawyerly.

Summer and Joy smile at each other. Not with the polite smiles that Kia's introduction has merited, but wide, excited smiles.

"Glad you like the van. Want to see it?"

"Summer . . ."

"Just the painting, I mean. Wonderful dolphins. Done by a friend of mine who was on the tuna boat protests. You don't eat tuna, do you?"

"No," Joy says.

"Well, good. Because it's not fucking tuna. Not at all. It's dolphin. Beautiful dolphin. Dolphins can talk, did you know that? They fucking well can. Probably better than humans. Not that I think that's an excuse to eat tuna. Just because animals aren't cute doesn't mean . . ."

"I like noodles," Joy says. "Chinese noodles."

"Great. Noodles are good. That's one thing I hate about traveling. No good noodles!" Summer laughs.

"Do you travel a lot?" Joy's tongue caresses the sophistication of the word *travel.*

"Not that much. But I have to travel for my work. I'm a photographer."

Kia nods, observing Summer and Joy. If only Joy had been this engaged during the visitation with her mother.

"How did you start?"

"My mother bought me a camera. In fact, she bought it for me right over there." Joy and Kia look to the empty patches of green past the silver globe where Summer is pointing.

"Where?"

"Over there. By the Unisphere. In one of the gift pavilions. And she bought me this." Summer untangles one of her necklaces from the others and holds out the silver charm. "Recognize it?"

"It's a globe." Joy sounds disappointed.

"Any globe?"

"I don't know." Joy's voice verges on the petulant.

"Look around you, girl. You want to be a photographer, you gotta open your eyes."

"I didn't say I wanted to be a photographer."

Kia gives Summer a disapproving glance, but Summer is undaunted.

"Well, you want to be alive, don't you? Look around you and see if you see this same silver sphere anywhere."

"That thing?" Joy points.

"Absolutely. That's the 1964 World's Fair Unisphere, and it's still standing, right here in Queens. My mother brought me here. I must have been in about first or second grade. And she bought this necklace."

"It still fits you?"

"OK, OK, different chain. But the same globe. Pretty amazing, don't you think?"

What Kia thinks is that it is amazing that she never knew this before. Never really noticed the same seven silver continents jutting in the same way, and the same three silver strands like orbits that had been photographed with a lens open the entire night. Never knew.

Joy nods, transfixed.

"But the Brownie camera was the absolute best. It made me become a photographer."

"What do you take pictures of?"

"Rocks. Animals, mostly. I love animals. That's what I really do, besides being a photographer, I'm an animal rights activist."

"Wow. Cool."

"I don't think we can ignore animals. I'm thinking about having another airbrush on the back. A wolf or something."

"Summer—" Kia tries to interrupt, but when Summer is this electrified, it is difficult to divert the current of her conversation. It makes Kia impatient. But it also, as Kia realizes again and again, makes Kia envious. Summer has an enthusiastic faith that Kia believes she herself lacks. This isn't the reason she loves Summer, Kia knows, but it is one of the things that Kia finds irresistible. Even as she is annoyed.

"Or a giraffe. Probably not a wolf, at all." Summer smiles. "And not a dog either. Probably a giraffe. Yes, a giraffe would be terrific on the van, on the cargo door. The fifth door, they call it. Which sounds kind of mystical, don't you think? Especially since there are only three other doors. I mean, I mentioned that to the car salesman when we bought it, but he said real determined that the door in the rear is always the fifth door, no matter how many other doors there are. The fifth door in a four-door van! So maybe that's why we usually don't call it that. Or the cargo door either."

"What do you call it?"

"The way back."

"That's weird." Joy nods her head.

"Kind of," Summer agrees. "But it's not the back. The back is just behind the front seats. We took the middle seat out when we bought it. So, there's lots of back. Good for carrying things. Big things." Summer winks at Kia. Both Kia and Joy pretend not to notice. "No, this is further. Behind the back. The way back."

Summer is opening the fifth door, the cargo door, the way-back door, the hydraulic spring sighing, revealing the space big enough for a series of five filled grocery bags, or a huge suitcase, or a person to fit.

"Nice," Joy is saying, when Kia sights Ms. Swedlowe the social worker walking by the fountains that surround the Unisphere. Kia nudges Joy and points.

And Joy runs toward Ms. Swedlowe.

Kia suppresses a spurt of jealousy. Joy should be lingering here, Kia thinks, with me, her damn attorney. Rather than running toward some simple social worker. And a heterosexual one at that. She should be staying by me, letting me walk her over to the social worker and transfer custody. At least saying good-bye to Summer, who she seemed to be glued to a moment ago. Kia's jealousy now threatens to erupt on behalf of Summer.

"Well, at least the social worker showed up," Kia says brusquely. She graces Joy and the social worker with a desultory wave. Debates whether or not to go over to them. But Joy seems intent on the social worker in a way that Kia hasn't seen before, even more intent than Joy seemed to be on Summer, and certainly more intense than Joy was when she was with her mother.

"The wolf's in the car," Summer whispers, demanding Kia's attention.

"I guessed. Is everything OK?"

"Fine, though it probably has to go to the bathroom. We should walk it before we get started. The park is as good a place as any."

Kia nods, nervous. "Got a leash?"

"Of course. I've got everything we need for a trip to Quebec. Even have your toothbrush. And a few clothes."

"Did you bring that backpack of stuff I put out?"

"Yes, oh my organized darling." Summer laughs. And kisses Kia on the shoulder. Takes her hand and leads her to the side door—the third door—of the van.

Sliding this door open, undoing the latch on the plastic animal carrier, and getting the leash back on the animal.

"This wolf looks kind of pathetic," Kia says. The animal doesn't look as wild as she had thought it would. It isn't snarling, though she thinks it might.

"Say *dog*." hisses Summer.

Summer tugs on the leash, but the animal doesn't respond.

"Nice *dog*," Kia says, with what she hopes is a coaxing tone.

There's a long moment when Kia senses something must be going on between the animal and Summer, though Kia couldn't say what it could be. Finally, the animal lumbers out of the van. Summer and the slinking wolf-dog walk toward the wide cement path, the one that circles the fountains which encircle the Unisphere.

"I hope we're not going to try to make it all the way around. The poor thing looks unnerved."

"Our dog will be fine," Summer says, though she doesn't sound so sure.

"Summer?"

"Yeah?"

"I never knew that necklace was from here."

While Kia is waiting for Summer to answer, all her attention being siphoned by the possibility that Summer's lips might move, Joy Parker is on the other side of the Unisphere, one of the figures camouflaged by the sprays of water, coming full circle.

And even if Kia weren't still waiting for Summer to say something, goddammit, Kia was too far away to see the social worker, Ms. Swedlowe, hurrying away from the globe and from Joy Parker, alone but not for long, because soon she will be in the front seat of her boyfriend's car, that beautiful red car, kissing him and being kissed, deeply, and deeply appreciative of that nice attorney Kia Townsend, who offered to take that pesky Joy Parker back to the foster home.

Wherever Summer goes, she is a tourist. Not only because of the cameras, now tucked under the driver's seat, but because she has polished the attitude of a spectator. She looks and looks and sometimes she even sees.

Even on the New York Thruway.

Even in the dark.

Sometimes she sees pages from books, exhibits in museums, a slide in a class on contemporary art history at the University of South Carolina. Summer had taken the class because Kia, her new roommate, had signed up for it. Kia had said that she liked the way *contemporary* and *history* balanced each other, and maybe could even cancel each other out. Art beyond time.

Driving down Utopia Parkway, Summer will inevitably point out the house of Joseph Cornell, a reclusive artist who made surrealist shadow boxes, and she'll launch into a description of one of his works. Sometimes one of the ones about ballerinas. Or one in homage to Emily Dickinson. Or one with a parrot.

And now, at Lake George—at the signage for the exit for Lake George—Summer launches into a description of what she sees. The photographer Alfred Stieglitz and the painter Georgia O'Keeffe. It is 1923, 1926, 1930. The way Summer talks, time is just another dimension of space: It's as if Summer could take the exit onto Route 9N and drive the van right up to Stieglitz's driveway and see him taking a photograph of O'Keeffe painting "Lake George Window, 1929."

To listen to Summer's descriptions is to almost believe that Lake George exists only because of Stieglitz and O'Keeffe, as if they made it real as well as famous. Gave shadows to the birch trees that the trees would otherwise lack. Painted the lake blue. Kia remembers the class. Remembers that she took better notes and got a better grade. But she does not recall the slides with Summer's intensity; does not recall the slides at all.

Summer's memory often startles Kia.

Summer's memory, Kia thinks, is so good because it is so recent. It begins in college. It begins after the lawsuit. It begins the day she gave her mother a certified check for half of the settlement from the man who was her father. It begins the night she stopped soaking in the bathtub and stopped combing her hair. There is so much room in Summer's memory because everything before that has been evacuated.

Or so Kia thinks.

Or so Kia likes to think.

Not because it explains the fact that her lover has such an annoyingly good memory, recalling the damn slides from some stupid college course on contemporary art or art history or whatever it was, but because the alternative is ugly.

Kia doesn't like to think that Summer remembers what the man who was her father did. Kia doesn't like to think that Summer remembers that he touched her in the same places that Kia touches her. Kia doesn't like to think that Summer might be like any of the kids that Kia represents, like the one raped by her older brother, or the one with the four-tine scar across his nose from a hot fork, or like Joy Parker, that adolescent chained to a radiator because she liked another girl.

Summer's fragments connect, as they so often seem to, into something between a chant and a rant: "that protean sky, these green fucking green hills as red."

Past the sign for Lake George, Kia finally interrupts: "Weren't those utopian communities around here too?"

Summer sighs. "No, not around here, dear. Your sense of geography sucks! You must be thinking of somewhere else. Niagra? No, Oneida. Yes, Oneida. The Perfectionists."

"Perfectionists?"

"Life is perfectible. But the fuckers couldn't make a go of it. Gave up."

"What happened?" Kia asks, wondering whether Summer learned this in college, in some course Kia doesn't remember taking. Kia has to resist all over again being dazzled by what Summer knows. Or what Summer seems to know. Kia never checks what Summer says; it could all be lies.

"What happened was the usual," Summer hisses. "Their own ideas killed them. They said they believed in charity. And they did."

"So, that's awful?" Kia starts laughing. "You mean, they all had nose jobs and became movie stars and that's what they named their kids and the kids grew up to be dykes?" Kia's words are garbled by her own laughter.

"Getting tired?" Summer reaches across the stick shift for Kia's knee. "Besides, that's not 'charity' that you mean."

"Whatever." Kia is still laughing at her own joke.

"Seriously, charity was their demise. Charity is based on inequality. You know, like charity cases. So, they were always being charitable and acting so fucking superior."

"I know the type." Kia shakes her head in the dark. Bites her lip. Opens her mouth anyway to say: "Think they're movie stars." And starts laughing again.

"You can laugh, but you know it was the animals that caused their failure. They raised animals. Treated their animals like shit. Charitable shit, but still shit. Like goddamn products, like commodities. Sold them. And so, of course it couldn't work. Humanism never does."

Kia is still giggling, but she closes her eyes to sleep for a while as Summer keeps driving north along the dark highway.

*T*hey say that dogs do not dream.

They say that wolves do not dream.

Therefore, wolf-dogs do not dream.

Or if these animals do dream, they dream only of this: chasing something (dogs: cars and cats; wolves: deer and caribou; wolf-dogs: humans). That is why the legs of these animals twitch in their sleep. They are dreaming of chasing something and their legs twitch because they are not smart enough to know that they are only dreaming.

In the plastic carrier, in the back of the van (but not the way-back), the wolf-dog's legs twitch. But it is not dreaming, not sleep-dreaming anyway, because it is awake. Very, very awake.

Awake enough to smell the synthetic roof of its carrier and above that the steel of the van and above that, the dark, dark of the sky. Awake enough to hear the fibers quivering in the blanket beneath it, and the silence of the floor of the carrier, and the vibration of the floor of the van, suspended between axles, and the dark, dark of the macadam. Awake enough to feel the two humans to the north, talking and thinking, and the one human to the south, sleeping, her leg twitching, as if she is dreaming of chasing something, or of running away.

*K*ia loves to drive. She doesn't get to do it often anymore, living in Queens, living with Summer, but she still loves it. Loves wielding the shield of the steering wheel. Loves riding the clutch with her left foot and giving commands with the scepter of the stick shift. Loves putting a cassette tape simply marked "Kia" into the cassette player, turning the volume knob, and singing.

She knows she will not wake Summer. Or if Summer does wake, Summer will only smile. Despite Kia's untrained voice, its rawness unmitigated by any natural talent. Despite Kia's favorite songs, copied onto the tape labeled "Kia."

Kia's colleagues at work, who all think they know Kia, would think that they would know Kia's favorite songs, the ones she would put on a cassette tape of her favorites. Or if not the precise songs, at least certain genres, certain artists. There would be progressive folk, a bit of Tracy Chapman, perhaps some Ferron, and certainly Sweet Honey in the Rock. For a slight edge, there might be some Melissa Etheridge and even some Patti Smith. One of her white colleagues at work is certain that there would be at least one song by K. D. Laing. This colleague would be even more certain of her choice if she knew what Kia remembered about her father. Kia as a child, waiting for her father to come home after working the night shift at the paper mill so she could kiss him good-bye before she ran off to school. Kia's father, a working man in north Florida who couldn't join the country club—even if he were the factory owner instead of the alternate-shift supervisor—because he was black. Kia's father, neglecting his mother's gospel and his brother's jazz in favor of Patsy Cline. Kia remembers Saturday mornings, when her father would play "Crazy" on the record player that he called the victrola. Kia's favorite, though, was "Walkin' After Midnight."

One of her black colleagues at work is certain that there would be at least one song by Queen Latifah, and one by Aretha. This colleague would be even more certain of her choice if she knew what Kia remembered about her mother. Kia as a child, waiting for her mother to come home so she could tell her mother about her exciting day at school. Kia's mother, a very blond and very white woman who worked as a waitress at the country club that Kia's father couldn't join. Kia's mother, disowned by her own mother, her own father, and everyone except her younger sister, who was no longer allowed to listen to Elvis Presley, for fear that she too might descend down the slippery slope that had been Kia's mother's path to damnation. Kia remembers Saturday mornings, her mother making biscuits, turning up the volume on the kitchen radio by the third bar of any Sam Cooke song. Kia's favorite was "Frankie and Johnny," because she always thought of the lovers as being women, in disregard of the actual lyrics.

Summer, unlike Kia's juvenile attorney colleagues, knew these things about Kia. Just as she knew the song on the cassette tape now. "Free Bird" by Lynyrd Skynyrd.

A band of redneck, white-boy rebellion. Nothing there for black people or women, but Kia loves them. Loves the *wang-wang* of their electric guitars. Loves the fuck-you lyrics. Then it was called Southern rock and now it is called classic rock on the radio stations that still play "Free Bird" at least once a day. Kia knew people who knew the Van Zant brothers, core members of the band, from Jacksonville, Florida, Kia's hometown.

"Free as a bird," Kia croons.

Like all Lynyrd Skynyrd fans, Kia mourns the plane crash that took Ronnie Van Zant's life and destroyed the band, right after the release of their album *Street Survivors*, which showed the band members engulfed in flames. Kia remembers that. Though she doesn't remember what she was doing when she heard the news of the plane crash. Whether she was still in Florida or not. Whether she had gone to college and seen Summer in the bathtub.

Summer remembers. Remembers October 20, 1977, when Lynyrd Skynyrd's Convair 240 airplane crashed into the swamps near McComb, Mississippi.

And Summer remembers Patsy Cline's untimely demise in a plane crash near Dyersburg, Tennessee, in 1963. And Summer remembers Sam Cooke's mysterious death in 1964, in a shooting incident in Los Angeles. Though Summer knows she cannot remember those things. She was not there. Not in Mississippi or Tennessee or Los Angeles. But she remembers. Remembers certain details.

She must have read about them somewhere.

She must have.

Kia's voice breaks, every time, when she hits the note for *bird*, although it is not an especially high or demanding one. She does a little better on her accompaniment of "Frankie and Johnny" and a little worse with "Crazy."

Saturday early, early morning, not yet light, little traffic, and the flatness of Interstate 87 lulls Kia into a series of mental detours until she is thinking about law school. She isn't remembering. Not recalling the studying in bed next to Summer's steady sleeping or the exams that seemed like endurance tests as much as anything else or the intoxicating smell of the highlighters she used on the expensive textbooks. She is thinking. Thinking about what law school has meant to her life.

She knows, of course, that law school doesn't have a single meaning. She knows that it has meant different things for different people. For some, it was nothing more than executing a blueprint: They had simply walked up the aisle and found a good job at their family's law firm waiting for them at the altar. For others, it was the means to accomplish a dream: They had struggled against the odds and were now judges or professors. And for others, it had been just a way of filling up time and attempting to fill some void that yawned at the end of college.

Without legal ancestors or ambitious dreams, Kia knows she seemed like just another time filler, a void avoider. But that's all surface. There's something else. Not just Summer and the inspiration of Summer's lawsuit. Not just a steady job and maybe even the chance to help people. There's something else.

Something difficult to describe. If she were writing a self-help book, she could call it self-esteem. If she wanted to talk to Summer about it, she would call it bravery. If she listened to her mother, she might name it either sass or chutzpah.

But whatever it should be called, it was this: That she, a black-white girl from some Florida swamp, could look any official in the eye, calm and slightly superior and totally in control. Even if she was driving a torn-up van with a psychedelic dolphin airbrushed on the side. Even if her lover was slumped in the passenger seat with one of her many earrings half caught in the torn fabric of the upholstery and one of her many feathers sticking straight sideways so that she looked like a cartoon "injun." Even with an illegal animal crouched in a carrier meant for large dogs and not wild wolves.

Even if all of those things were true, she could look at that very nice, very blond, very official male face and answer his routine inquiry about the purpose of the visit to Canada and say simply "holiday." And smile.

And not falter in that long moment as the official looks at the van and at Summer and the dog carrier in the cargo area.

"Have its shots?" the official asks.

"Certainly. You want to see the papers?" Kia is prepared for class, prepared for court, prepared.

"Not necessary," he says. And almost smiles back.

And waves her on.

That she—Kia Townsend, attorney at law—can drive across the border, into Canada, into Quebec, where she is trying to imagine how the signs will look in a different language, a language she does not know. Even if those stray sounds she has been trying to assign to the wolf-dog are not the wolf-dog but are—as she suspects—human. Yes, even if it's true that huddled in the way-back is a runaway. A girl who was her client and who had been chained to a radiator and who is probably listed among the missing by now by law enforcement.

This is what law school meant. What she learned. Not only that she could probably be charged with kidnapping the girl. But something else. Something like competence. Something like belonging to the system. Something like privilege and how to pretend she had always possessed it. Something like faith in her own powers.

from signs in Florida such as PALMIER QUÉBÉCOIS or ARBRE FRUITIER at the entrances to trailer parks near Winter Haven and Frostproof and Hesperides. She had been riding with her mother and her mother's boyfriend in the red truck, and when she had said something about the signs, intending only to talk to her mother, he had snorted as if she had been talking to him. He spit his words, words like Canuck and Canadian and snow-bird, as if there were something disreputable or threatening about the retirees who came to Polk County, Florida, each Thanksgiving and stayed until Easter. He had even called them frostbacks, laughing at his pun on *wetbacks*, although neither Joy nor her mother had returned the laugh. Joy had wondered if the man driving the red truck knew that some of her mother's friends had called him a wetback; she figured he probably did.

And although Joy knew that a *palmier* looked like any other palm tree and an *arbre fruitier* like any other fruit tree and that the trailer parks of the Québécois really looked no different from other trailer parks, Joy somehow expected everything to be altered now that the border was far behind. It was sensible that Florida wouldn't change with a few labels, but after all, this was a whole different country. A foreign country. And foreign countries were exotic.

So, of course, an *arbre* would look different from a tree. And it did. For the *arbre* were often silver-trunked, unlike the trees of Florida, certainly, and unlike the few trees she could remember from New York. Yes, they were different. Silver.

Though in her heart of hearts, as her mother Loretta would say, Joy knew that it wasn't the change in the alphabet from *arbre* to *tree* that accounted for the difference. Otherwise, the *palmier* would have looked different from the palm trees that had surrounded them. No, it was something else. Though what that something else could be, Joy could not say. Though the wolf-dog must know, Joy thought. Watching it watch her through its one blue eye.

"Don't stare at the dog," Summer said, as if she had been

The clouds and corners lighten first, turning into night gray, then slate gray, then pearl gray. Eventually, the morning sun and a few clouds, bloated and lonely, combine to cast huge shadows. Perfect silhouette etched on the bumpy lavender canvas of the Laurentians, the *Laurentides*.

Even if Kia and Summer were going to argue—about the girl Joy, now sitting in the cargo area of the van instead of hiding in the way-back and probably the object of a police search; about the wolf-dog, now sitting on the floor outside of the carrier which Summer had moved to the way-back; about the directions to Havre de Loup, which commanded a turn to the *oest* or east or west or *ouest* at the sign for RESERVE FAUNIQUE DE LAURENTIDES—the landscape would not allow it.

The neat road is bordered by baskets of flowers, hung from cast-iron poles that seemed to serve no other purpose than to suspend the baskets of pink, red, yellow, and purple above the asphalt. Small houses appear here and there, in rectangular clearings, and the land that faces the road in front of these houses is invariably overflowing with flowers of all different sorts, even tulips. It is a place where summer is a deep breath, as long and as necessary.

Looking out the window, Joy notices the baskets of flowers and the smallness of the houses and the faces of clouds on the mountains. But mostly Joy looks at the signs, trying to read them. Rehearsing them to herself so that she would be able to speak the required language. Remembering bits and piece watching Joy. Although she could not have been. Summer was watching the gentle road, watching for signs to the place they were going, on some loop, near some fantastic reserve, east or *ouest*, probably all the way to the silver tundra.

She had thought the ground would be white. A silvery, magical white. So far north that winter could not be more than a breath away. Where the snow would be so lush it would cover everything she could see now with a cold innocence. And everyone would agree that it was beautiful because there was no alternative.

She had thought the house would be white. And it was. Although it was difficult to tell which building was the house and which building was a barn and which building was something else. For the three white buildings revealed no hierarchy, no order, no red shutters announcing *house,* or wide red doors announcing *barn,* or red roof in such disrepair that the only conclusion could be *shed.* It seemed lucky, though, that after such a rutted path, rocks barely crushed to make the road, the van's metal sloshing against itself as it navigated toward Havre de Loup, there was a clear place to park. The blue van airbrushed with dolphins coming to rest comfortably between a respectably rusting yellow Suburu with Manitoba plates and an orange American car that she eventually recognized as a Ford Pinto.

She had thought the women would be white. Or had not thought—which was the same. Default: white. Even her. The same person who had loved the tragic tones attached to the word *mulatto* until it had been applied to her by a well-meaning teacher, until her mother said it was a cheap word. And anything cheap, in her mother's vocabulary, was evil.

But the two women approaching the van are not white. A third woman is sitting on a picnic bench, brushing her long Asian-black hair.

Kia and Summer and Joy clamber out of the van. They are tired and stiff and bleary-eyed. It is Saturday late afternoon, and they have been in the van for twenty hours.

Summer laughs at the sign in bold red letters: CHIEN MÉCHANT. Bad dog.

"Come on, bad dog," Summer says to the wolf.

At Havre de Loup, the women tangle in the short yard, which drops off to a dry streambed completely clogged with rocks. The bed is wide and on the other side are young, misshapen trees. The placement of the rocks, like the shape of the trees, is a consequence of flooding last year.

The wall of woods is broken by a slender path through the wilderness that seems to lead to the tops of the mountains. Over the mountains, a mist hangs and circles the highest, darkest trees. That must be where the wolves live, thinks Joy, wonders Kia.

"It's a small area, certainly," one of the women is saying. "Small for wolves anyway. Tiny for creatures who used to roam huge areas, traveling three hundred miles in a week."

Larger than a backyard in Queens, Joy thinks, Summer says.

"Mmm."

"How many wolves are there now?"

"Not sure. Ten to twenty."

"Do you think there will be problems with a new one? Will they let her join the pack?"

"Don't know. And don't know if there is only one pack."

Kia, who likes the idea of a lone wolf, doesn't say anything, though she wants to. Wants to say something for Joy Parker's sake, but is not sure what that something would be.

"Well, we'll soon see," Summer announces.

"Not right now. The new animal will stay on this side of the streambed for a while, in a very large pen. The door of the pen will be kept open, with food available in the pen. Then we hope she will go up the mountain."

"And if she doesn't?" Joy asks.

"Then the wolves will come and get her."

*T*he women are still outside, the Saturday afternoon sun slanting hard on the mountain as if in battle with the mist. But there is something relaxed now. Now that the wolf-dog is in her temporary pen. Now that Summer, and Kia, and Joy have been invited to stay the night, in a building that had seemed like a barn but was actually a nice space with a bathroom. Now that Summer has gifted the women with two fine bottles of French Pouilly-Fuissé.

It is Joy who wants an explanation of how the women came to have Havre de Loup. Joy wants one of the women to have been saved by a wolf as a child. Or read wolf stories by her grandmother. Joy wants logic, cause and effect, a progression, an explanation. Joy is an adolescent, waiting for her own life to reveal its plan, as if she and her life were somehow two distinct creatures, as if she were a shadow of her own life, lurking around and following it in through the woods.

But why, why did you do it? Joy asks this.

Charity, a woman answers in French. What else can one do but have charity?

Is that the same reason Kia does what she does? And Summer, bringing the wolf-dog here? And is that the same reason Marisa kissed her? No, it can't be that, Joy thinks. Because she still confuses charity with pity. Which is not what the woman meant.

Yes, charity, Josephine continues in her thickly accented

English, the Canadian lilt at the end of each sentence an invitation to her listeners to nod their heads in agreement.

Josephine, named, she is explaining, the same as every third woman in Martinique, the same as Napoleon's beautiful wife, Josephine, whom he stole from the island of beautiful women, Martinique.

"The beautiful island of beautiful women." Josephine sighs.

Joy, who has most recently lived closest to Martinique—although the peninsula of Florida is in fact far from the Caribbean island, it is certainly a lot closer than Quebec—asks the obvious question:

"Why did you leave Martinique and come here?"

"Oh, that is an interesting question." Josephine's eyes glitter at Joy in a way that might be interpreted as teasing.

"Let me tell you. Yes, let me tell you my beliefs. I believe that just like every person, every place has a soul. The people who are lucky are born in a place which matches their souls. And their souls become more and more refined by the place.

"They are unlucky, though, because they remain ignorant. They think that they love the place because they were born there. They call it home and they think that explains their attachment.

"And so those of us who are unlucky, we must search for our homes, for the place where our souls match the soul of the land. But we are lucky too, for our search takes us places we might never go, lands which we thought exotic and foreign, on the maps and inside of ourselves. And when we find the place, we are happy—more happy than happy—because we know it could be otherwise."

Joy and Summer and Kia have been nodding. They are still nodding, although Josephine has finished talking. She is folding her hands and looking up toward the mountain at the thickening mists.

Summer and Joy are silent, and so it is Kia who responds. It is Kia who sums up what Josephine has said, as if Josephine is a witness who might later testify and Kia the lawyer wants to be sure that she has understood Josephine correctly. It is Kia who says: "Then what you're saying is that you left Martinique to look for your home?"

"Oh, no," Josephine laughs, "I left Martinique because I murdered a man."

*T*he women and almost-woman, Joy, are sitting around the rectangle of an outdoor table, caressing their plastic glasses of iced tea. Perhaps because Joy was still a student or perhaps because Blanche Saint-Claire was a teacher, or perhaps because it was a Saturday evening just after the end of the academic year, their conversation has drifted toward school.

Or perhaps Josephine started it. By telling the story of a reporter from Montreal who had wanted to write a story about Havre de Loup but kept calling it *École de Loup*—school for wolves! As if wolves needed a school to be wolves. Though, maybe, she said, they did. At least the wolves who hadn't been educated by their pack. Perhaps there was need for an academy. Forget sanctuaries and havens, think *lycée*!

"And how would they be tested?" Joy wonders, almost surprised that she has spoken aloud. Her own voice sounds strange to her, as if she has picked up a French accent.

"How might you think?" Blanche says in her Miss Saint-Claire the teacher tone.

"Well, not multiple choice," Joy answers. "Those are so unfair." She is thinking about her last test, the one before she had cut school with Marisa and gone to the ocean, the one before she had been chained to the radiator. She is thinking about a specific question, one she thought she had answered correctly. But had been wrong.

9. The natural vegetation of North America:
   A. has not changed much in the last 500 years.
   B. was changed rapidly by Native peoples.
   C. has changed greatly since the year 1500.
   D. has become mostly forests and grasslands.

She had picked A. Because how could the land change? The land was the land, wasn't it? But the answer was C: changed greatly since the year 1500. And then she had remembered the teacher saying something about the European settlers clearing everything and turning forests into farms. Maybe it was even in the book, though she hadn't really been reading it. In Florida, her mother had sometimes helped her study and she hadn't ever failed a test the way she did now. No, then her mother had sat across from her at the tiny table in the tiny trailer and had asked her questions from the textbooks. Or when it was very hot, they had sat outside and her mother propped the book on her knee and quizzed Joy. But now it wasn't like that. Joy had even asked her mother for help, but her mother said Joy was old enough to study by herself now. But Joy knew that wasn't the reason her mother wouldn't study with her anymore. The reason was Queens.

Kia's parents had always helped her with her homework. Success was important. They told Kia that change had come and things were going to be easy for Kia. Segregation was over. The future glistened.

Amid all that shininess, there must have been days she learned something other than how to keep quiet, how not to be noticed, how to avoid the black girls and the white girls and the boys. How to sit perfectly still during social studies, which meant current events. And current events in this large Southern city could only mean one thing: race. Another debate on school desegregation. Another report on the relationship between the federal government and the states. Another fight in the girls' gym, which the principal would characterize as a "near race riot" and suspend everyone in the interests of what he called fairness.

Kia told her guidance counselor she wanted to take graphic arts. The students did etchings in linoleum blocks. Silk screens. A photographic plate. The guidance counselor laughed. Girls don't do graphic arts, he told her. Girls take home economics. Learn how to cook a poached egg and sew an apron from a pattern and bathe a beige plastic doll. It was important for every girl, no matter her color, to learn to bathe a beige plastic doll.

So Kia went to the principal, who probably assumed Kia was there with some complaint about some comment by some white teacher, and may have been surprised at Kia's request, which would explain his answer: "Yes, I don't see why not."

After that, the black girls and the white girls and all the boys avoided Kia even more than she avoided them, once in a while whispering "bulldagger" or "faggot" or "pussytaster" in the hall as Kia was on her way to graphic arts, where she was learning how to make the most precise cuts with her X-acto knife. Where she was resisting inhaling the silver gelatin, or placing it on her tongue, just to taste its power.

Summer, in the seventh grade, had to do a report on an explorer. From the list of explorers passed around by Miss Finch, her social studies teacher, Summer chose Champlain, mostly because it sounded like *champagne*, which was something that Summer knew her mother ordered for the annual New Year's Eve open house hosted by Mr. and Mrs. Chocolate. And because Champlain was one of the few names that remained by the time the list got to Summer, the other students having selected the ever-popular Christopher Columbus as well as Marco Polo, Hudson, Cortés, Magellan, and Vasco da Gama.

Summer, in the seventh grade, researched and wrote her report on Samuel de Champlain, the explorer known as the "father of New France" and founder of Quebec. Summer preferred the books in the adult section of the town library, outside of which there was a plaque to honor the generosity of

Mr. and Mrs. Chocolate. Summer, in her very best handwriting, wrote:

> At forty, Samuel de Champlain returned to Paris from the New World and married a *fille* (girl in France) named Hélène Boullé, who was aged 12. She had a dowry of about $1200 in gold and her parents were impressed that Champlain was a famous explorer and there was a marriage contract that said Champlain now had to pay her expenses and everything even though in consideration of her "tender age" the bridegroom would not consummate the marriage for at least two years unless her parents agreed. Later, they did. They had sold her already, so it didn't really matter. Hélène probably did not like this at all, because Champlain may have been famous and everything but he was just a smelly old man to her. He probably tried to give her chocolates and other candy, but she was rich already and lived in Paris, where everyone had candy. After a while, he left to go back to Canada and explore some more. He came back to Paris, though, and made her go to Quebec with him, but she hated it. It was 1620 and though she had ladies-in-waiting, she was pretty lonely. She stayed there four years and hated every minute. Though Champlain said she hated the long winters and the absence of the excitement of Paris (in his book *Voyages*, 1632), she probably really hated him and his smell and that he never let her walk alone in the forest and kept consummating the marriage although it had already been consummated in Paris before he left the first time.

Miss Finch, the seventh-grade social studies teacher, had to grade Summer's report. And Miss Finch—who had taught in Chocolate-town for many years, had taught Summer's mother, in fact, and had been at the ceremony at the library at which the plaque was installed, acting along with her "spinster roommate," the librarian, and everybody else in the whole stupid town as if Mr. Chocolate were as wonderful as he pretended and not the ugly, ugly person everyone who had ever worked for him (which was mostly everybody, one way or another) knew he was—did the only thing she could do. She gave Summer the highest grade she ever did, a 99 out of 100. (Miss Finch always said that perfection was unattainable.) And she would have given Summer her blessing, if she had believed that blessings, like perfection, were possible.

Although she had believed it was possible—she had!—that Summer would grow up to sit around a rectangular table in Quebec, with her lover (yes!) and two other women and an almost-woman, talking the way women do, waiting for the reward of a wolf howl, feeling as whole and as happy as any person on the planet could. Though it would be perfect if Summer had a better haircut; Miss Finch herself always had a modified bob. Gradually stippled with silver.

Like the hair of Blanche Saint-Claire.

Like the fur of the wolf-dog, outside in its wolf-dog pen.

Like the sunlight lingering on the dried sugarcane stalks. Josephine working in the fields in Martinique, when all she wanted then was to go to school, any school, no matter how cruel with nuns, so that she could learn to read. Then she could learn more about the strange things she had heard about from her brother, who was at an *école* in Port-au-France. She could read about real things, things that really mattered, like snow and maps of huge continents and werewolves who sucked blood from babies.

Some people, like this woman who had been sitting at this same table when Summer and Kia and Joy and the wolf-dog had parked their van, seem to welcome every new acquaintance as an audience for the story of their lives. Joy and Kia are listening to Eden and her sandpaper. Eden has swung one leg over the gray bench and is rubbing the portion in front of her, making the gentle circles she would make if she were massaging a horse, as she describes her birth as if she remembered it. It was a beautiful summer day in Seoul, the sun reaching toward noon, when her mother squatted in back of the brothel, wishing for her own mother, far off in a northern village. The other prostitutes admired the baby that she was, such light-colored hair and crisp eyes, though everyone agreed that her mother had to do the only thing that she could do. At the Amerasian Adoption Agency, Eden's mother signed some papers with a small mark, an ideogram for *wolf*, although of course there were no wolves in Seoul and this was not her family name. But she thought it was the baby's father's name, for he had had a tattoo of a wolf on his bicep, and she thought the baby's father would claim the baby at the Amerasian Adoption Agency, although how she could have fooled herself into thinking such a thing was hard to imagine.

She was adopted by a minister and his wife in Norman, Oklahoma. Her new mother and new father never talked about Korea and had never been there and soon it seemed as if Eden had been born in the Norman General Hospital along with all the other children she knew. It even seemed as if her long braids were going to be blond when she looked in the mirror, but they never were.

Eden laughs at this, looking at Joy and Kia, who smile in compliance. Summer joins them on the bench, her own blond hair looking like a badly woven wicker basket fending off the rays of the sun.

Summer gently places a backpack on the bench beside her and pulls a camera from it.

"Put that away," Kia scolds.

"Kia doesn't like having her picture taken." Summer winks at Joy.

"Summer. Not here."

"The light's fine."

"Summer."

Summer looks alarmed by the squeaky irritation in Kia's voice. Sweet, sweet Kia, Summer thinks, does not usually interfere with her photography. Kia has even helped her do outrageous and dangerous things, like setting up a tripod on a slender outcropping of rock, and that time at the beach when Kia could have drowned. So what's the problem now?

"Summer," Kia repeats. "Does the word *evidence* mean anything?"

"Oh, OK. Makes sense." Summer puts her camera away as gently as she had retrieved it. Actually, it didn't make all that much sense to Summer—how would anyone ever get her prints anyway and connect them to anything criminal?—but Summer tries to humor Kia's lawyerly side. Unless she has no choice, of course, like breaking into the animal shelter.

"So," Summer fills the silence, "what's been happening?"

"I'm just boring them with the story of my life," Eden answers.

"It isn't boring," Kia reassures her.

"Well, then, I guess I'll go on."

Joy nods.

Summer squints.

"I went to college to study ecology, at the University of

Oklahoma, right there in Norman, but there wasn't much in ecology, although the meteorology department is excellent. Tornadoes." Eden laughs again.

She says she thought she would be a park ranger, although she did not meet the height requirement, even thought of bringing a lawsuit about that, but then decided to go to graduate school at Boston University, in marine biology. Which is how she came to be here, at Havre de Loup, invited by some woman she calls Collie. Not far from the St. Lawrence Seaway, not really that far. She landed a fellowship to study whales, the right whale in particular, it's the subject of her dissertation. Which she's writing right now. At least when she isn't watching the wolves come in and out of the fences or sanding the old picnic table benches.

Eden blows the dust from the bench and scoots back a little farther, resuming rubbing the long neck of the bench.

If Joy were to ask a question, she might ask about the parents in Norman, Oklahoma. Or her years as a teenager there. Or if Eden had ever been in love with anyone, another woman with long blue-black braids or even a man. Or why she is in so far from the ocean if she's interested in whales.

But Joy doesn't ask anything. Because Eden has explained everything. How all her roads led to Havre de Loup. How her life has the logic of a map, dotted with inevitable continents. Yes, Eden is one of those people who has lived to demonstrate that her life is shapely.

And then there are other people, like this woman called Madame. That's it: Madame.

It has made Kia think she must be a ballet teacher or something.

A sign of respect or something, Joy assumes.

Though Madame does not seem to return the respect. For whenever the currency of stories is brought out from pockets of conversations, Madame excuses herself and none too politely. A scowl mars her small face and she squints as if the sounds of people's voices are giving her a headache. Her walk away from them is brisk and her back so straight as to be disapproving.

But, of course, by absenting herself from the commerce in stories, she conveys, at least to Joy, that she has the most valuable story of all. For everyone knows that the best story cannot be traded; it is a secret.

Though if Joy dared to ask Madame, the woman would say that she is hiding nothing. That she has nothing to hide. Which is not the same as desiring to tell everything. Or desiring to listen to other people tell what they pretend is everything. Or even something.

Madame, even if she had stayed, would not have been interested in the most interesting of the stories told last night in the kitchen, stories about education, and knowledge, and learning, although Madame would say that she is deeply curious about all of these things. Madame, like Blanche Saint-Claire, is a teacher. Madame, like Blanche Saint-Claire, teaches language.

French. Madame has been conjugating the verb *être* for nearly thirty years. It hasn't changed. It is still *je suis; tu es; elle est; nous sommes; vous êtes; elles sont.*

Although for a brief time it seemed as if it might change. It might have changed and Madame would have been the one to make it change. And perhaps she did. For some women. For some women who read French and some women who read Madame's works in translation.

Women like Kia and Summer.

For there was a different story Kia and Summer could have told last night in the kitchen. A later story. Not about Kia ditching home economics for the romance of an X-acto knife, or Summer in social studies writing about a French explorer's marriage to a twelve-year-old. A subsequent story. Summer and Kia in college. Together. In the same class.

The class was not contemporary art.

The class was "Women's Utopias."

One of the required books was Madame's book.

One of the required essays on the take-home final: to discuss whether the novel was utopian or dystopian. The correct analysis, as any student who had attended even half of the lectures knew, was a defense of the novel as utopian. A refutation of the dystopian reading as misogynistic.

Summer, fashioning herself an outlaw, made the dystopian argument. She focused on the harm the women had suffered before they had banded together; she mentioned their brutality even as she claimed it was necessary self-defense. She argued that life should be better. For Summer, despite everything, could not accept that utopia would be grim.

The professor gave Summer a grade of B.

Kia, who did not fashion herself an outlaw and was still trying to please everyone, nevertheless usually said what she thought to be the truth. An essay exam was no different. And so Kia wrote that the novel was neither utopian nor dystopian. Kia wrote that such an either/or choice was meaningless when confronted with the complex society of the novel. Kia concluded that the author was trying to communicate different possibilities, which were neither good nor bad, which just were.

The professor gave Kia a grade of C. The professor had not yet heard of deconstructing binary oppositions, which was what Kia was doing although she had never heard of it either.

Madame, however, who was living in France, had heard of such things and was thinking about deconstruction even as she wrote her great novel, which she thought of as neither utopian or dystopian, but just an attempt to create a world with words.

Which is the opposite of what she wants to do now.

Precisely and exactly the opposite, the critique of binary oppositions be damned.

Madame is weary of words.

Or that is one version. Weary, which is a polite way of saying *bitter*. Bitter because although she is a well-known writer and her books have been assigned to students for twenty years and people recognize her name and she gets invitations to lecture in several countries, she teaches grammar. The grammar of a language she deconstructed. She is teaching people to conjugate *être*. Of course she is bitter.

But there is another version. In this version, Madame's books are still assigned to students and she gets invitations to lecture and she teaches grammar and *être* is still conjugated *suis; es; est; sommes; êtes; sont*. But this version has no bitterness, although it does have weariness. The weariness of words. Of narrative.

Of the imposition of order.

Of the useless egotism of thinking one creates the world with words.

Madame once believed, like all her contemporaries—hell, one of the first of all her contemporaries—that language constructed reality. What a convenient theory for one who valued language above all else! And it could be political as well. Simply by making the language less woman-hating, one could make the world more woman-loving. Yes, Madame believed that. Was one of the first who believed that. The strength of her belief—no, the communication of her belief in words so well grafted together, there was no room for doubt—

made others believe. The others who purchased her books and assigned them to their students and wrote damn dissertations about her use of language to alter reality. Some woman who is now a professor somewhere, probably in the States, got her damn Ph.D. analyzing Madame's analysis of *être*. And that professor, like most of the others, probably still believes.

Still believes that to write *je suis* is to constitute the self. Madame no longer believes.

Yes, Madame is bitter in this version of the story also.

And this story is also a story that Madame finds useless because what she no longer believes in is the power of narrative to deconstruct and reconstruct the world.

Luckily, there is a third version.

Which is the version Madame would tell if she believed in telling.

The version that explains how she came to be living at Havre de Loup. For in this version, where she lives is the important part, not what she does for a living. *Here* is the privileged theme of the narration, not *teaching grammar to a bunch of québécois teenagers.*

And in this version, Madame is one of the many women who abandoned careers that others envied. Madame is one of the many women who no longer believe that language is the ground of being; that being would be even if there were no word *être* in its various conjugations. There are women like Madame all over the world. Living their lives instead of describing them.

Though Madame remains a theoretician. Perhaps even a recalcitrant utopian. Which explains the reason Madame is living her life at Havre de Loup when she could be living it in Montreal or Marseilles or Martinique.

It is de Loup.

Madame's old colleague and once lover and often rival and now landlord, Collie, is also pursing the wisdom of de Loup. Collie is in the Arctic, writing Madame long letters about her adventures looking for the white wolves. She recounts a sight-ing of the wild wolves, white and ferocious, running across the tundra. Despite her attempt to move beyond language, Collie cannot resist the narrative impulse.

Collie's letters imply that Madame is too feeble to track through the Arctic like a real wolf-woman; that Madame has chosen the pampered route, which of course will reveal no truth. Collie's letters reek with her belief that struggle produces knowledge.

Madame no longer reads Collie's letters. Not since the letter in which Collie wrote that she felt as if she were tracking her own imagination across the tundra of patriarchy.

Madame is not interested in Collie's imagination or in the tundra of patriarchy.

Madame is not even interested in the wild wolves of the Arctic.

Because they are wild.

Instead, Madame is interested in the wolves and wolf-dogs of Havre de Loup.

Because they are not wild.

Because they are feral.

It is the only hope, she thinks.

*T*he women go inside.

Summer and Kia.

Josephine and Blanche.

Eden.

And even Madame.

Joy, the almost-woman, does not.

The women sit at the kitchen table, telling stories not for information now but simply to amuse themselves. Madame listens with her arms folded. Though perhaps she laughs once in a while.

Sunlight still drifts through the windows and it seems as if it's almost midnight before twilight comes.

"The shortest night," Eden says.

"So far north. Quebec, Quebec," Josephine says.

"*Entre chien et loup,*" Madame says. The time between the dog and the wolf, between night and day. Twilight.

They hear the howls. Sounding as sarcastic as the moon at noon, but then softening somehow. And as if the howls aren't all vowel, as if they could be translated into language, each woman bounds the sound with words.

Madame would hear the verb "to be," and Eden would hear the wind in Oklahoma, and Summer hears the photograph she wanted to take out there in the yard and Kia hears the song Lynyrd Skynyrd would have recorded if they had lived.

And Josephine hears blood. The rush of it from a man's belly, less than she thought it would be, really more from the hand with which he had tried to block her knife, but she had always been quicker than he was, and their mother had always made her chase and kill the chickens, never him.

They listen to the howls.

The night sounds weaving other melodies.

Frogs, maybe. Crickets?

So that when the scream comes, it sounds almost as if it is a part of the evening symphony, an off-pitch note of the howl.

Summer is the first one out of the door, into the yard, her mouth sucking the word *Joy* from the wolf-dog's music.

The trees are black but in the gaps beyond them, there is still a sweet lavender light. Look at the light, Summer tries to tell the wolf-dog. Stop looking at the girl.

The girl with sunglasses on. Still. In the twilight. Sunglasses.

"Take off the fucking sunglasses," Summer yells to Joy Parker.

But Joy has been transformed into a portrait in a *tableau vivant*, as incapable of motion as an image in one of Summer's photographs.

The wolf-dog is also inert, but its stillness vibrates with temporality. Everything will change in a moment, the wolf-dog's electrified fur seems to proclaim.

Everything.

Summer flattens her hand.

Approaches from an angle that will put her body between the girl-woman and the wolf-dog.

Don't be a dry stream.

It's a voice inside her head again. But it's her voice this time.

The wolf-dog turns toward Summer, twitches its ears.

Kia, standing near the door, wants to scream. Wants to howl. Wants to run to the van and get a gun that isn't there from the way-back and murder that animal. Wants to wake up back in Queens, near Utopia Parkway.

Kia watches as the wolf-dog draws itself into a crouch, ready to pounce.

Summer stands.

"Wire," she says.

Out loud.

Joy can hear her.

Tilts her head.

"Take off the fucking sunglasses," Summer says again.

Joy's hand is at the stem of the sunglasses, pulling them from her face.

"Don't move," Summer commands.

Then Summer howls.

Summer howls like a wolf.

It makes Josephine think of werewolves.

It makes the wolf-dog flatten its ears. Walk back to the open door of its pen.

Dry stream, Summer hears.

And maybe Joy hears it too. And maybe Kia and Josephine and Blanche and even Madame.

Summer sleeps with her hand cupping her crotch. Usually her left hand, but sometimes the other one. As if to catch something that might seep from her, some dream or some slash of blood. As if to deflect.

Kia sleeps with her hand resting on her forehead, palm outward, as if she is an exotic heroine in a silent movie, demonstrating her distress. The effect spoiled only by the reminder of a smile, teasing the fullness of her lips.

The wolf-dog sleeps with its eyes open. Both the blue one and the brown one. If what it is doing could be called sleeping. Its head resting on its paws, its ears flattened against its skull.

Josephine and Blanche sleep curled into each other.

Eden dreams.

Madame does not sleep, but sits on the side of her bed, thinking of Collie in the Arctic, who is not sleeping either, but writing another letter to Madame.

Joy sleeps on her stomach, her hipbones pressing into the mattress, her shoulders hunched backward into the covers. When she was much younger, she thought of her bed as two slices of bread waiting for her—she pictured herself as a piece of delicious American cheese—to slip into position and create a sandwich. Now that she is older and has kissed another person, she thinks making love will be like that. Or she dreams it will.

Summer's pretty brave, isn't she?" Joy is standing near the streambed early Sunday morning, invited by Kia for a walk. An invitation Joy didn't think she could have refused.

"Brave? Oh. I don't know. Stubborn, certainly. And good with animals."

"I don't think the wolf would have killed me."

"I don't either." Maimed, maybe, though Kia doesn't add that. Doesn't add any of the terrible scenarios that had performed themselves in her mind throughout the night. Doesn't add anything about her own worries, would never share the vast weight of her responsibility for the entire situation.

"But it looked pretty wild."

"It was probably the sunglasses."

"Yeah. That's what Summer said. And I did see that guy on TV wearing sunglasses."

"Which guy?"

"The guy that beat the wolf. There was a TV story. I saw it."

Kia flashes on a paragraph in Joy Parker's abuse and neglect petition about the television near the radiator where the girl had been chained. The petition that she needs to talk to Joy about. Joy, her client. Though if they ever get back to Queens, it's doubtful that Joy will be her client. Just as it's doubtful that Joy—who is still just a kid, after all—will be able to keep her mouth shut about Havre de Loup, about Quebec. Which makes it doubtful that Kia could continue to be a juvenile rights attorney, or possibly an attorney at all.

Though Kia, the ethical attorney, knows it is her client's choice. So Kia starts to advise Joy about her options. Stay here. Go back.

One day to decide: today. Sunday.

"We have to leave by dark," Kia apologizes. "I have to be back at work Tuesday morning."

Joy nods her head as if she understands, but she has that sullen stare that all of Kia's clients seem to quickly perfect.

*J*oy is more verbal with Summer. "Tell me how you did it," Joy commands.

"Did what?"

"Your parents." Joy is fishing near the dry streambed, putting together fragments she has heard to shape her bait.

"I didn't do anything. They did it to me."

"But you did something back."

"The court part was easy. There wasn't even any court. It wasn't like I thought it was going to be, like a book or TV. I mean, it wasn't *Perry Mason.*"

"Who?"

Summer laughs. "Oh, that's probably before you were even born. Perry Mason was a famous TV lawyer. Always won his case. Not only won but blew everyone else out of the fucking water. It would be in the courtroom, the last five minutes of the show. The true criminal would confess and Perry Mason's client would walk. My mother loved that fucking show. She'd watch reruns and make me sit between her knees while she brushed my hair. She was always brushing my hair."

"Is that why you don't brush it now?" Joy touches her own hair.

"Hey, kid, watch your mouth. I wear my hair this way in solidarity with the endangered animals of the world."

"Sorry."

"And because my mother was always brushing it."

Summer's wide smile emboldens Joy: "But you haven't told me how you did it."

"I was trying. Until you didn't know about Perry Mason."

"And now I know. TV lawyer who always got his man."

"Right. And like I said, it wasn't like that. We didn't go to court or nothing. I thought that Mr. Chocolate—that's the man who was my father and was fucking me just like he'd done my mother—would just break down on the witness stand and admit everything. Because, of course, Perry Mason would be defending me! But I didn't have Perry Mason. I had a feminist. And Mr. Chocolate had every lawyer on the East Coast. So, we didn't even go to court."

"You lost?"

"Did I say that? I didn't lose. I won. The old man caved in. Settled. Called it blackmail and all that jazz but he paid up. Didn't want bad publicity. Some scandal like that could ruin the image of the product. I mean, you wouldn't want your kids eating candy made by a child molester, would you? And then there was his precious wife. Didn't want her to know. Like she didn't know already."

"So you got a ton of money?"

"Not a ton, but some. Put half in the bank and gave half to my mother."

"To your mother?"

"Sure. I figured she'd been messed up just as much as I had. And I also figured that Old Man Mr. Chocolate was going to kick her out. Though he didn't."

"He didn't? Where is she now?"

"Still living in the servant's cottage where I grew up. Still cleaning the house for Mrs. Chocolate."

"What did she do with the money?"

"I don't know and I don't give a fuck."

"You don't ever see her?"

"Nope."

"Do you miss her?"

"Yeah. But I don't miss the person I am when I'm with her."

"What do you mean?"

"I don't like myself when I'm with her. She taught me to be quiet and not make a fuss. She taught me I was worthless just like her. She taught me to feel like shit."

"But she couldn't help it, could she?"

"Maybe she couldn't, maybe she could. It doesn't matter."

"Yes, it does! She was only teaching you to be like that because that's how she was. Because that's how she lived and thought you should be like that too."

"You could be right, Joy Parker. But I have to say I don't care."

"You have to care. The reason someone does something matters."

"You sound like Kia when she's being a lawyer. It matters in court. It matters about guilt. You can say someone was excused or justified. I know all that. And I know your mother probably chained you to a radiator because she truly and sincerely thinks it's for your own good, just like my mother told me to shut up when my old man, who I wasn't supposed to know was my old man, fucked me. But I'm saying, it don't matter to me. I'm saying I'm not deciding whether or not the woman is going to the electric chair—I'm not a damn attorney, I'm a photographer."

"How come I've never seen your pictures then? If you're famous?"

"Don't get snotty. I never said I was famous. And I bet you couldn't name ten photographers if you tried."

"Edward Hopper." Joy isn't sure where she has heard this name, maybe from Summer herself.

"He's a painter." Summer softens. "But I did take an almost-famous photograph. Of a rock. A silvery round rock that looked like a globe almost. I called it Join the Struggle for Happiness. I wanted to name it Utopia, but Kia came up with Join the Struggle for Happiness and so that's what I named it. And people liked the photograph because of the name. The world wants to be happy. You can tell that from the land. Look at that sky. Those rocks in the dry streambed. The wolf-dog deciding whether or not to leave the pen. All wanting to be happy. The

Buddhists say the rocks want nothing. That the lack of desire is happiness. And maybe they're right but I've never seen that. Even Mr. Chocolate was struggling to be happy. Thought that fucking some fourteen-year-old would make him happy. And your mother. Thinking that keeping you inside and away from your girlfriend would make her—and you—happy. And my mother, thinking if you don't say anything, the world won't take away that little piece of happiness you've managed to hide."

"Yeah, I guess." Joy nods. "But don't you feel bad? What about Christmas? Don't you miss your mother on Christmas?"

"Christmas? What's with Christmas, Joy? It's one fucking day."

"Well, you don't miss her because you have Kia. She's your Perry Mason, isn't she?"

Summer laughs again. "No. Not my Perry Mason. Kia is my utopia."

*I*t's almost noon when Josephine and Joy find themselves alone together. It hasn't been easy. Neither wants to seem obvious, as if she is scoping the other out like a potential date, but then again, the possibility that they might live together at Havre de Loup does make each want to know more about the other.

What Josephine wants to know are things that can't really be asked. Are you a *bon enfant* or *gamine*? Neat? Honest? Will you do your homework? Will you take to the language? Will you complain of the winters? Will your nightmares disturb me more than once a week?

What Joy wants to know is what she asks: "Did you really murder a man?"

"*Entre nous? Qui.*" Josephine looks directly into Joy's pale eyes.

"What happened?"

"You want the whole story? I am no raconteur."

Joy doesn't know what Josephine has said, but she shakes her head up and down and tries to smile encouragingly.

"I killed a man. With a machete to his stomach."

"Why?"

"My brother was a *roué*. A lecher."

"You killed your brother?"

"*Oui.*"

"Why?"

"He went after my friend. My friend Collie. And so I killed him."

"You must have loved Collie very much."

"No. *Amourette.* Eh? Puppy love."

Joy has never liked the term and makes a face.

"Is *verité.*" Josephine adds, "But it was *difficile.* I went to a *voyant,* a fortune-teller, and she did tarot and told me that I would be killed if I stayed. Men do not like a woman who kills men. *N'est-ce pas?* So Collie brought me here. To another one of her projects. And then she left."

"I thought you came here with Blanche."

"Ah. She came later."

"Why?"

"To be with me. She left the island of beautiful women to be with me."

Joy nods with all the solemnity that envy accords.

On the other side of one of the white buildings, Blanche is watering the potted plant she will take back inside at the first sign of frost in September. She is looking at the second-day bloom, knowing that tomorrow it will be shriveled and the day after discarded by its stem; she stares at it as if it is a hot-pink funnel that can pour her into the other side of her life, the way her life might have been. Her life would have been continued among the huge hibiscus bushes of her home, always covered with blooms, so that when one flower dropped off no one noticed, there were so many others to take its place.

Hibiscus, in every color except blue, her mother always said, because blue already claimed the sky and the water. A blue hibiscus would have revealed blue's greed and the other colors would have rioted with resentment.

Though there was a hibiscus of the deepest purple, almost as deep as night, because night has never been afraid of judgments about its rapacity.

And a lighter purple, lavender almost, *crépuscule*, the color of twilight romance. The color of the blossom her mother gave her when Blanche left the island of beautiful women to follow a beautiful woman to this land as cold and as stunning as silver.

PART THREE: JOY

*T*he sky is my mother. Clouds across her face. A sun in her corner, more blond than even the most ambitious promise from one of those small dark bottles. A moon that waxes and wanes, like love.

People don't understand the sky, don't understand her. Think the sky is being cruel when it thunders, when it strikes out with lightning, killing some guy who was just standing under a tree on a golf course, killing some woman who was digging organic garlic in her carefully tended garden. People don't think about the four-iron, the galvanized trowel. Don't understand that the sky only does what it thinks it has to do. Don't understand the sky like I do, like a daughter.

Here is what Josephine said: that my mother loved me. That mothers love their daughters. That women give their daughters names of love. Joy. Summer. And Josephine, the most beautiful woman on the island of beautiful women.

I felt bad then for Kia, but when Kia turned her head in that certain way she has, Josephine added her name to the list. And explained that in her language, which isn't French at all but something very different, *Kia* was the name of a beautiful bird, a bird that no one ever captured.

I saw Miss Saint-Claire open her mouth as if she were going to say something, but then close it again.

Blanche, Josephine said.

Which means white, I know, though I don't see how it could be loving to give such a name to such a dark daughter.

"She is like the clouds," Josephine said.

And I guessed it made sense.

Yes, Josephine seemed to know what it's like to be a daughter.

Summer doesn't understand because she is refusing to be a daughter. Left her mother, left her hair to go to a jungle. Loves a wolf more than her mother. But then, her mother did let that man touch her. My mother would never let that happen. She's asked me about it a hundred times, but it's never happened. And if it did, I know my mother would thunder. She would strike that guy dead. That's what my mother would do. She's not like Summer's mother; she loves me.

Kia doesn't understand either. Kia tries to be so cool. "Nonjudgmental," I know she would call it. She says it's my decision. Says she's only my attorney and that I'm the client and that I'm in control. Like I have a choice. Like I could go back to some foster home and see my mother in the park by the big globe.

Or like I could really stay here. Like I could be a child again. Raised by wolves.

A long time ago, back in Florida, back in school, I read a story about a kid raised by wolves. It was a boy-kid, because the interesting stories are always about boys. It was supposed to be a true story, because the unbelievable stories are always true. I wish I could remember it better. I wish I could remember something other than the fact that the boy howled at the moon. He pointed his mouth to the stars and the animal sound spiraled up and the sky funneled down, or at least that is how I imagined it. The humans caught him and did experiments on him, but he wasn't happy away from the wolves. He couldn't use a toilet. He couldn't sleep in a bed. He kept breaking out of the beautiful boy-bedroom where they had imprisoned him so that he could sleep under the sky.

I think the sky is the key. If I could just return to the land where I know the sky. If I could convince my mother to take us back. To Florida. Where the sky is wide and real. Where there are no radiators to be chained to. And she—and I—could blame all the trouble on New York, on Queens, on a place where neither of us could see the sky and so we got lost.

Or I could stay here. In the North, in a different language. And the sky, the mother of wolves, could be my mother. Not Josephine or Blanche. Not Kia or Summer. No, the sky could be my only mother.

*T*he sky is my lover. I place my body between the ground and the sky, and the sky is on top of me like a blanket, like a lover. All soft and open.

I heard them talk about money. And it made me feel dirty. I heard Kia and Summer and Josephine and Blanche Saint Claire discuss my "upkeep." I hid and I heard them and it hurt. It sounded like charity.

Like the foster mother who gave me soup from a can and crackers as if it were a great favor to feed me.

Like my mother's boyfriend when he gave my mother money for school supplies.

Wherever I go, I'm a charitable case. But at least I have some choices. I can stay, just like Kia said. I want to be realistic. If I ever want to see Marisa again, I must be realistic.

I heard them talk about staying themselves. Staying here with me. At Havre de Loup.

Summer had suggested it. Told Kia that she thought that the place had room for them. For them and their new lives.

"It's like a women's utopia," Summer had said, "what you've always wanted."

"Me? I like civilization," Kia had snorted.

"What's there to like?"

"I like my job. Our apartment. I like Lorenzo's Restaurant and the garbage along Utopia Parkway. I like our life."

Summer had stalked off then, as if she were angry. And maybe she was. Though she was smiling.

Smiling as she went over to Madame. The two of them sitting silently for a while.

I would like to ask the woman called Madame what she thinks. I would like to ask the woman named Eden. I would like to ask the woman Collie who owns this place but doesn't live here. I would like to ask each of them what she thinks about this place and about love.

Whether love is a place.

But instead I have to ask the sky.

If the sky were my lover we could go on a trip together. I could take her into a restaurant and we could have a long conversation about our plans for our future. There would be flowers on the table and we would bend our faces close to them and pretend we were kissing them so that we could smell their softness.

If the sky were my lover I could take her to the ocean.

A beautiful ocean without syringes stabbing through the foam of the waves. An ocean with whales. An ocean where the wolves come to sip the salty water.

An ocean that is a mirror to the sky. A lover.

*T*he sky is an ear. A funnel hovering over the earth, sucking all the sounds into its bony clouds of funny shapes: a hammer, an anvil, a stirrup. The three tiny bones in the ear; a multiple-choice-test question. Correct.

The inner ear provides balance. There is fluid navigating its way through a complex labyrinth. I wondered how the fluid never got lost. I wondered what the fluid was. Water? Blood? I never asked questions in school. And there was no test question on this.

The sky listens to the wolf-dog howl. Howl as she tries to decide which pack to join. There must be more than one pack. There must be more than one choice. Like I have.

I can stay here.

Or I can go back.

I can stay here at Havre de Loup, learn French, listen to wolves, write Marisa and have her come visit me.

Or I can go back to Queens, go to court, kiss Marisa, convince my mother to take me and Marisa back to Florida.

One of these choices must be closer to utopia.

I pronounce each one out loud.

First one.

Then the other.

The wolf-dog howls from high on the mountain, outside of its pen.

The other wolves answer.

It's twilight.

It's almost dark.

I can see Kia and Summer by the van, pretending to check the engine and the tires and the fifth door.

When I finally tell the sky what I am thinking of doing, I am hoping the sky loves me enough to answer me, to whisper its agreement or disagreement in my own ear.

And the sky does:

Love me;

Whisper deep in my own ear;

Agree with my decision.

acknowledgments

Portions of this collection, often in different versions, have appeared in the anthologies *Night Bites, Night Shades* and *Out for More Blood*, and the periodicals *Blithe House Quarterly, Harrington Lesbian Fiction Quarterly*, and *Kalliope*.

In addition to the editors of the above, especially Victoria Brownworth and Judith Stelboum, I would like to thank my smart editor, Keith Kahla, my supportive agent, Laurie Liss, and my insightful and careful critic, Sima Rabinowitz. For their contributions to the life beyond these pages, I am grateful to George Demetri, Samuel Singer, Gail Shepherd, and as always, S. E. Valentine.